AND

YOU

INVITED

ME

IN

a Novel

AND
YOU
INVITED
ME
IN

Cheryl Moss Tyler

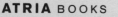

ATRIA BOOKS
New York London Toronto Sydney

ATRIA BOOKS

A Division of Simon & Schuster, Inc.
1230 Avenue of the Americas
New York, NY 10020

BEYOND WORDS
PUBLISHING

20827 N.W. Cornell Road, Suite 500
Hillsboro, Oregon 97124-9808
503-531-8700 / 503-531-8773 fax
www.beyondword.com

This book is a work of fiction. Names, characters, places, and incidents either are products of the author's imagination or are used fictitiously. Any resemblance to actual events or locales or persons, living or dead, is entirely coincidental.

All scripture quotations in this publication are from the *Holy Bible, New International Version*. Copyright © 1973, 1978, 1984 by International Bible Society. Used by permission of Zondervan Bible Publishers.

Editor: Terra Chalberg
Managing editor: Lindsay S. Brown
Proofreader: Marvin Moore
Interior design: Sara E. Blum
Composition: William H. Brunson Typography Services

First Atria Books/Beyond Words trade paperback edition January 2008

ATRIA BOOKS and colophon are trademarks of Simon & Schuster, Inc.
Beyond Words Publishing is a division of Simon & Schuster, Inc.

For more information about special discounts for bulk purchases, please contact Simon & Schuster Special Sales at 1-800-456-6798 or business@simonandschuster.com.

Manufactured in the United States of America

10 9 8 7 6 5 4 3 2 1

Library of Congress Cataloging-in-Publication Data

Tyler, Cheryl Moss.
    And you invited me in : a novel / by Cheryl Moss Tyler. — 1st Atria Books/Beyond Words trade pbk. ed.
        p. cm.
    1. Homosexuality—Fiction. 2. Christian conservatism—Fiction. 3. Brothers and sisters—Fiction. I. Title.
PS3620.Y585A83   2008
813'.6—dc22

                                                                            2007019722

ISBN-13: 978-1-58270-166-0
ISBN-10:   1-58270-166-0

The corporate mission of Beyond Words Publishing, Inc.: *Inspire to Integrity*

TO MY HUSBAND, MICHAEL,

AND OUR DAUGHTERS,

ELIZABETH AND MICHAELA

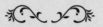

He heals the brokenhearted and binds up their wounds.

Psalm 147:3

AUTHOR'S NOTE

THIS IS A TRUE STORY. It's true in the sense that it's still happening every day in many conservative Christian communities. The character of Annie could be my neighbor who hasn't had the courage to tell anyone her brother died of AIDS, and the character of Alex could be your brother.

This story belongs to those who live in fear that their homosexuality will be discovered by their devoted church friends and family. This story belongs to the thousands who can't comprehend why there's a problem and who want to understand the conflict. Finally, this story belongs to the religious families and friends of gay men and women, and to the good people in conservative churches who want answers for how to reach out but have never had a road map to tell them how to get there.

Acknowledgments

MANY THANKS TO Bridget O'Brien, without her none of this would be possible. From the time she read the manuscript, Bridget knew this book would give a voice to people who had no voice, and the cries of their hearts would finally be heard.

A special thanks to my husband, Michael, for encouraging me to write a novel. To my precious mother, Lucele Moss, whose love for writing has always been an inspiration. To Denise Rome, who read countless rough drafts and was always there to brainstorm ideas.

To Lois Liles and my church family for their constant prayers. To Dr. William Moss and Dr. Steven Standaert, who read the drafts and supplied medical information. And to Mae Argilan, Janean Bollinger, Claire Dees, Connie Dillingham, Harriett Edwards, and Valerie Lomax.

Finally for friends who have died from AIDS and whose church fellows did not respond when needed. And for Bruce Sonnenberg, who envisioned what the church could do for persons with HIV and AIDS by creating the church-based ministry He Intends Victory with the hope that no one will ever be forgotten again.

PROLOGUE

"Before I formed you in the womb I knew you . . ."

Jeremiah 1:5a

SHERATON, CHICAGO
FRIDAY, JUNE 1, 2007

An overflow crowd filled the room for the Christian Women's Club annual spouse night banquet. The clatter of dishes was drowned out by lighthearted conversation. A gentle voice broke through the noise.

"Tonight our keynote speaker is Mrs. Annie Whitley from Hallton, Wisconsin, a small town in Waupaca County just west of Green Bay. Thirteen years ago God worked miracles in the Whitley family. They were willing to live transparent lives in a challenging situation. Open your heart to her incredible story."

Those attending were quick to applaud as the master of ceremonies stepped back and gracefully extended her hand toward Annie. After getting to the podium and breathing in the fragrance of the flowers, Annie began her talk.

"For decades conservative Christians have considered homosexuals our adversaries. I'm not here to ask you to accept this lifestyle, but instead I've come to tell you a simple story of unconditional love. I forgot about undeserved favor—what we call 'grace'—when I first learned that my brother, Alex, was gay. My husband and I were offended by Alex's union with his partner, Scott. Yet when we quit dwelling on the outward aspects of their relationship, God changed our hearts. The lives of people associated with us were transformed as well.

"It was late summer in 1981 when my brother believed that God had given him a scripture for a family friend named Jett Taylor, the NFL quarter-back. Jett was in Green Bay getting ready for a game, when Alex felt an urgency to see him. What happened that night set a course that forever changed our lives."

THE COURSE IS SET ∽ 1981

Professional football was alive in Green Bay. The August heat had been unbearable during the New York Giants' afternoon practice. Hours later the odor of sweaty bodies still lingered in the hotel hall. The night before the first exhibition game was always stressful, but even more so when they weren't on their home turf. A knock disturbed Jett Taylor as he studied game strategies. As always he shared a room with his lifelong best friend, Harley Hamilton. Jett and Harley had played together on the same team in high school, college, and since they were drafted into the NFL in 1978.

Sitting on his bed, Harley motioned to Jett that he'd take care of the intrusion. The handsome running back with the cocky swagger walked across the room to open the door. Only Harley's dark blue eyes gave away the shock of seeing Alex Marshall outside their room.

"Why, Alex, what a surprise! Come on in."

Alex, the son of their high school football coach, had always been terri-fied to be in their presence. He looked across the room at Jett and almost for-got why he was there.

"Jett, I want to share something from the Lord." His mouth was dry.

Jett lunged for the door to shut it, but Harley stopped him while he was still in midair. Jett turned the full intensity of his gaze upon Alex.

"What do you mean you want to share something from the Lord?" His voice seethed.

"Tomorrow's the game, Jett. Just stay cool man," Harley said, and then he turned to Alex. "Leave and everything will be okay. I'll walk you out to your car if you want."

"Shut up, Harley. It's between Alex and me." Jett was like a rabid dog.

Harley glanced at Alex one more time. He then uttered a heavy sigh as he grabbed a towel to go for a swim and left through the open door.

Alex's heart rose to his throat once Harley was gone. He felt like he was a child instead of twenty-five years old. Any other time he would have been grateful for Harley's offer, but tonight Alex knew he had to deliver this message to Jett.

"As I prayed, Jett, this is from the Bible, uh—this has been a burden for several days now . . ." Alex felt such a desperate urge to share and at a complete loss for words.

"Look, Alex-boy," Jett's index finger poked him hard in the chest, "I know what you're burdened by: You're queer. Harley and I are very aware of it."

"What? This isn't about . . ." His words didn't come out as rehearsed. "I've been agonizing over you in prayer and I'm here to tell you what I believe the Lord has . . ."

"Don't say another word. You're lying about God just like you lied to get up here to this floor. Now, take your wimpy fag body out of my room." Jett redirected his remarks to the growing group of onlookers gathered outside the room. "Or was this just an excuse to get into my bedroom? Hey, guys, do you want to touch a fag?"

Alex ran, fearing what the group might do if he slowed. Jett's words were seared into his brain. It was only when he got into the safety of his car that he could finally think.

Why was I there in the first place? Alex asked himself.

For at least two weeks Alex had felt something terrible was about to happen to Jett. As Alex prayed, he gained compassion for his lifelong rival, but it was coupled with a sense of urgency to share a specific scripture. The verses said nothing more than a person is known by God before they are born. Alex perceived Jett needed to be reminded that God loves him.

"I thought I could trust you, God." His voice was barely audible even to himself. "I only talked to Jett because you wanted me to."

Alex felt betrayed. It was that obvious all his prayers were a joke. Tonight had shown him that he did not want to spend eternity with the people who tormented him. Soon after he was out of the parking lot, Alex turned on the radio to get his mind off what had just transpired. The news was on.

"... and those are Speaker of the House Tip O'Neill's remarks about President Reagan's economic plan. In the gay districts of major cities in America, the lights have gone out. In an announcement from the Centers for Disease Control in Atlanta, America is on the verge of a catastrophe in the gay population with a disease called GRID, which stands for gay-related immunodeficiency disease. It could be at epidemic levels by the end of the 1980s. The CDC says a vaccine should be available worldwide in less than two years. Gay and lesbian groups are converging on Atlanta to lend support to the CDC in this effort...."

Alex heard nothing else. He pulled over to the shoulder of the deserted country road and parked. Burying his face in his arms, Alex cried tears that had been bottled up for years. Loneliness and isolation had ravaged his soul. The worst part was that the One Alex thought he could count on had let him down.

After a while he looked at the sky and asked, "God, why can't it work? Why don't I fit in?"

A thought came to his mind. He considered Jett's words as he remembered what the newscaster said. Alex would go to Atlanta to look for an answer to what had been tormenting him all his life.

ⅇ ⅇ ⅇ

Samuel sat down at his desk and put on his glasses. Turning on the desk lamp in his small office, he gathered his pen and paper to begin another letter. He heard his wife crying. It was not often she allowed him to hear her grief, but today was their son's twentieth birthday. It had been two years since he left.

Samuel knew this letter to his son, like the others, would be returned unopened. Maybe it was best to not send any more. Samuel wanted his son home, but only on his terms. Why had God taken so long? Had he not been faithful to serve the one true God all these years? These questions plagued Samuel. God should know it was time for his son to come home.

❧ ❧ ❧

It was late when Harley got back to the room. He had learned how to maneuver to keep from getting caught for not making curfew. He tossed the towel on the floor and spoke to Jett, who appeared to still be working on plays for the game.

"What did he say?" Harley asked.

"He tried to give me some saccharine dribble about God," Jett replied with disgust in his voice.

"Jett, you know Alex is always sincere about the Lord," Harley said with compassion.

Jett turned and met Harley's eyes. He didn't want this night to ever be brought up again. It needed to be erased from everyone's memory.

"Harley, I know what you've been doing. That towel isn't even wet because you never got to the pool. Don't cheat on your wife—she doesn't deserve it." Jett gave a little nod and went back to his work.

The color drained from Harley's face. He went to take a shower without saying another word.

PART ONE

❧ The Call ❧

It is easy to love the people far away. It is not always easy to love those close to us. It is easier to give a cup of rice to relieve hunger than to relieve the loneliness and pain of someone unloved in our own home. Bring love into your home for this is where our love for each other must start.

Mother Teresa

I

PIEDMONT HOSPITAL, ATLANTA, GEORGIA
SUNDAY, MAY 29, 1994

AFTER MAKING AN ENTRY, Dr. Moss flipped through the chart one more time and then closed the metal medical record and stared straight at his patient. "We almost lost you this time, Alex. The good news is that with assistance at home, I think you can be discharged by the middle of the week."

Turning away, Dr. Moss rubbed his jaw with his hand. Telling a man he had only a short time to live was always difficult.

"Alex, you know we're doing all we can. Your T-cell count is critically low." Dr. Moss studied the tiles of the sterile hospital room floor as he searched for some positive words. "However, I had one patient who lived eight months after his T-cells were as low as they could go. Bottom line is, don't give up."

Across the room, Alex's life partner, Scott, stood at the window aimlessly watching the traffic on Peachtree Road. This was Alex's third stay this year at Piedmont Hospital and it was only May. The gnawing in Scott's gut would not stop.

Think positive. Think good thoughts. Think healing. It will work.

Scott's meditations were interrupted when Dr. Moss began talking to Alex again.

"Here's the situation, Alex. Scott needs help at home. I know he can work from the house, but you need to find another person to be in a rotation of caregiving. Once those arrangements are made, we'll discuss your discharge. Okay?"

Alex remembered how his lungs would get well and then the stomach trouble would come. He never felt quite well enough to enjoy life like he had six months ago.

He saw Dr. Moss glance at Scott before he continued.

"I'm going to be frank; you'll need to get your affairs in order in the next few weeks, but that also means enjoying each other." Dr. Moss shook Alex's hand and walked out of the room.

Alex was hardly a shadow of himself. Before AIDS, he had firmed and built up the muscles on his six-foot frame. His chestnut hair had grown down to his shoulder blades and was always pulled back in a ponytail. With his keen brown eyes and poise, he was equally at home in the courtroom and on the tennis court.

Alex had graduated from Emory School of Law in 1985 and quickly gained the reputation as a tough trial lawyer. By 1990 Alex had become partner in a prestigious law firm. Steps toward a political career were in motion when Alex started getting sick. By the time he found out he was HIV-positive, he was seriously ill much of the time.

Alex's recent bout with Pneumocystis carinii pneumonia, called PCP, had cost him another eighteen pounds. His muscle tone was gone and he now weighed 115 pounds; with his height he was little more than a skeleton. The nerves in his body were raw; to walk was torture. His mouth was filled with candida that looked like miniature mushrooms and emitted a fermented smell. He had the black lesions of Kaposi's sarcoma all over his body. Looking in the mirror was more than he could bear.

Scott went to his bedside and sat down in a vinyl chair. He tried to speak, but the words were stalled by the lump in his throat. Regaining control before moist eyes would betray him, Scott whispered, "I'll call AID Atlanta to arrange for someone."

"Not this time. I'm going to call my sister. Annie has the right to come if she desires." Even with oxygen tubes in his nostrils, Alex could not get enough air and frequently paused to try to get more.

"What good will calling Annie do?" Scott implored. "Your sister wants nothing to do with our life."

"It's my decision," Alex snapped. "Annie doesn't know that I'm sick. It might make a difference in the way she feels about me."

Alex lay back on the pillow and gazed out the window. Speaking wishfully he said, "With all my heart I want her to accept me for who I am. Maybe she'll come."

Alex's mind drifted to his break from the life he knew in Hallton. He had denied his feelings for other men until he was twenty-five, fearing condemnation from his community and church. He didn't know anyone else who had those kinds of feelings. When he went to college there were guys people whispered about. Alex also knew these guys were stalked and harassed until they left college without warning. With a high-profile father, Alex had kept his thoughts and desires bottled up until the night he went to see Jett.

The move to Atlanta provided him freedom to be himself. While he flourished professionally, his personal life was made up of unwise decisions: barhopping, one-night stands, and abusive lovers. When Scott came along six years later his life finally settled down. He was so different from anyone Alex had ever met. This thought snapped Alex back to the present as Scott broke the silence.

"So what if you call Annie? What could she do? We need someone who's experienced."

"Annie could be at the house while you're at work. I want to give her the opportunity to come and maybe reconcile our relationship."

Scott nodded. As much as he hated to admit it, Scott understood.

"My parents would never come. I'm the last person on Earth my father ever wants to hear from."

Alex smiled. "A sister is nice because she doesn't get jumbled-up failure feelings like a parent."

"Okay, tell me what you want me to do," Scott said with a sigh. There was little he could do but go along with Alex and hope that Annie would say no.

"You'd better get going. I'll tell you more after I call Annie." Alex saw this was becoming too much for Scott. "You'd better get going. Don't you have a Gay Pride meeting in a couple of hours?"

"I've got someone covering it for the paper. Anyway, I'm helping Mrs. Anderson's husband build a ramp into their house. She'll be coming home next week." Scott spoke of their elderly neighbors. The wife had broken her hip earlier in the spring.

"You're helping him after the terrible things he's said about us? Even with the mysterious religious brochures against homosexuality that magically appear in our mailbox?"

"I guess I'm trying to be more like you," Scott said with a blend of kindness and admiration in his voice. "You know what you always say: 'Forgive and go the distance to show our enemies we care.' I decided it's time I do it, too."

"And lose your reputation of being the Ice Man?" Alex kidded. He smiled for the first time in days.

Scott's office nickname was supposed to have been a secret, but he once overheard his staff referring to him by that name and later shared it with Alex. Alex told him it was pretty accurate description of Scott's personality to outsiders: cold, unemotional, and inflexible. Scott preferred to think of himself as cautious, logical, and uncompromising in his beliefs.

"I'm not going to run my mouth about my life—I haven't gotten that free yet." Scott's eyes were playful. "I'm just thawing enough to go beyond 'only writing a big check to charity'—your favorite phrase about my benevolence. I think this experience will make me a better person."

"I'm proud of you," Alex said. "Grab some cash out of my wallet and let lunch be on me."

Scott started to object but decided against it. Alex had seemingly limitless generosity, and lately Scott felt he needed to acquire these traits. After grabbing a $20 bill, Scott said his good-bye and left the room.

Finally alone, Alex felt the specter of fear and despair filling the room like smoke. Alex didn't know how much time he had or if Annie would reject him. He wasn't sure if there was a heaven or a hell. Christianity seemed like a dinosaur to him—not the "love thy neighbor" part, but the legalism that did not allow room for him and Scott, or for his disease. No conservative Christian church would ever permit someone who looked like him to sit on a pew.

Annie. The name brought a flood of emotions. *Would she be as rigid now? Could she love me in this condition?*

He had to give Annie a chance to be with him. They had argued after their father's funeral. Their father had been a high school sports icon everyone called The Coach. For years after the funeral, Alex swore he'd never see Annie again. But now that he was dying, and he wanted to make peace with her. Time was running out.

2

AUSTIN MEMORIAL PARK✑SUNDAY AFTERNOON

THIS HAD BEEN THE ROUTINE for most Sunday afternoons since March. Samuel would grab fast food and go visit his wife's grave. She was the only one he could talk to, at least now. When Natalie was alive, Samuel always seemed to have something more important to do and was rarely home for dinner. In recent days, Samuel had taken to eating his evening meal at the cemetery and would sit in the car if the weather was bad.

"I'm going to Peru, Natalie," Samuel said as he took a bite of chicken. He was under the tree next to her grave, sitting on a folding lawn chair he kept in the car.

Samuel had not reached his mid-fifties yet, but he looked much younger. He was groomed like a *GQ* model—his blond hair was liberally flecked with gray, and the suit he wore cost more than most people made in a month.

"I plan on leaving around the first of July—I don't know when I'll be back. I can't figure out who I'll talk to when I'm away. No one else knew me like you ..."

He paused as he chewed. Across the lawn he saw a family bringing flowers to a loved one's grave. Samuel felt a pain in his heart. It had been coming almost daily since the moment Natalie drew her last breath. It was the pain of knowing what he didn't do for his wife of thirty-four years before she died.

Natalie never made their marriage difficult. She very rarely said anything to him to correct his actions. Every time he looked into her eyes, though, he knew he had let Natalie down. She had to suffer the consequences for his quick temper with Scott.

Just after her cancer was diagnosed, Samuel had made plans to go to Atlanta and apologize to Scott for everything. But the chairman of the elders, Gerald Eubanks, reprimanded him for even considering seeing his "sinner son." He and the rest of the elders advised him to wait for Scott to repent.

Samuel gazed at Natalie's headstone. "I really wish I had called him, you know."

More families were gathering at their loved one's graves on this Memorial Day Sunday. A sense of conviction hit Samuel.

"You were right all along; I didn't need to be so bullheaded." He searched for the words. "I thought he'd come home—honestly I did . . ."

He stopped and in a regretful tone said, "Well, it's too late now to reconcile. I don't see how God can fix this mess. Please watch over Scott."

He wiped his mouth and tossed the greasy napkin into the empty chicken box.

"Preachers like me have no one they can turn to for advice." He looked around at the people and then back at her grave. "Why didn't we just stay with a small church, Nat?"

ATLANTA ~ SUNDAY AFTERNOON

The building project had started out tense with their neighbor, but now Mr. Anderson was grateful for all Scott was doing. They had to take a break until a spring shower passed. Scott left to buy them a late lunch. Alone in the car, he was once again reminded that it was only a matter of weeks before Alex would die. Fate had dealt him a rotten hand.

Scott was almost thirty-three—five years younger than Alex. In 1979, he had come to Atlanta to attend Emory University. His journalism major led him to start an underground newspaper for the gay movement that had been gaining momentum since the Stonewall riots in New York ten years before. By the time he graduated, *The Pride Position* was the official voice for the gay community throughout the Southeast. Scott had also invested in similar ventures in other cities across the United States.

Because Scott was so well known in his community, personal topics were off limits to everyone except Alex. No one had figured out that his father was Samuel Phillips, pastor of the largest conservative church in the Southwest. And certainly no one knew the circumstances that kept him from going home.

While things began building at an early age, in the end it was his father who demanded that he leave. It was a month after high school graduation when he caught Scott in bed with the music minister from the church. Chad was allowed to leave the house, but the elder Phillips's anger raged at Scott. In his wrath, Samuel had slapped Scott repeatedly and ordered him never to return. Scott hadn't even gotten to say good-bye to his mother before he left.

Scott met Alex when a mutual friend arranged a tennis match in June 1987. The attraction was immediate. They were devoted and monogamous. One year after they made their commitment official, they bought a house in the affluent Morningside area of Atlanta.

Instead of attending the predominantly gay Metropolitan Community Church, they became members of an affirming mainline church active in social issues. Scott and Alex were good citizens and lived what they considered to be a good Christian life. However, that life would soon be over. Scott asked himself what they did to deserve this illness. He shuddered at the thought of having to spend these last precious days with Alex's sister.

A torrential rain was coming down as Scott pulled his Jeep into the KFC drive-through. He was unable to make a rational decision about Annie. Death was marching into his home, and he had as much power over it as he had of stopping the rain. He needed someone to help sort out the future that was racing toward him. His heart cried out for God to help.

3

PIEDMONT HOSPITAL～SUNDAY AFTERNOON

So this is the end.

Alex had never thought he would die so young. His final wish was to have Annie with him, but she might refuse. Their only contact since they argued after The Coach's funeral had been through the exchange of holiday and birthday cards with trite messages.

Thinking about the turmoil upset his breathing. Alex lay back on the pillow and put down the phone. He had to think it through one more time.

Their separation from each other was in the name of God. The Christian community calls it "disfellowship" when all compassion and support is withdrawn. It's like what the Amish do when one of their own becomes too worldly. For Alex, it was an attempt to force him to repent of his homosexuality and return to a literal interpretation of the Bible. Even with that, Alex wanted Annie to come. He lay back on the pillow and clutched the phone.

"Annie . . ." Alex spoke her name in the stillness of his room.

Annie was more than a sister. Their mother had died when they were young—he was barely seven years old. Nine-year-old Annie had taken his mother's place in the home as well as in his heart.

His mind drifted to the April morning when Annie had called him to say that their father had died. *Good riddance*, Alex thought as Annie asked if the arrangements were convenient for him. Alex wanted to bring Scott, which started an argument. To please his sister, he agreed to come alone.

Alex felt like a freak. People gawked at his long hair and then quickly huddled together to gossip about The Coach's gay son finally coming home. He had already decided to leave Hallton immediately after the funeral. But the worst came when his eyes briefly met Jett's. Alex thought about thanking Jett for giving him reason to leave Hallton after their encounter that night; Jett avoided him, though.

There were people who treated him with dignity—like Harley's parents and in-laws. Jett's wife, Donna, also made an effort. Alex wondered what had happened to Jett's first love, Rita. She was beautiful and hung on Jett's every word. Donna was different—somehow more self-assured than Rita had been. Alex was at peace as he talked with Donna.

After Donna left, Alex felt like a stranger in his home until he noticed his favorite high school teacher. She motioned for him to join her. Alex took his coffee cup and joined her at one end of the dining room table.

"You look great, Alex. I always knew you'd succeed once you got away from your father," Susan Spencer said. "But is it true you're gay?"

Susan was always direct with people. Alex felt safe answering her—she had been his strong ally at school and church with The Coach. It was her encouraging words about his academic abilities that inspired him to attempt law school.

"All my life I knew something was different. I didn't fit in with the rest of the guys." Alex made a gesture toward the former football players milling around.

"You have qualities that most of these men need," Susan replied.

"I wish Annie would see it and at least try to understand."

Alex caught a glimpse of his sister chatting comfortably with her friends. He longed to have her interact the same way with him.

"Annie's been under a lot of pressure. They had to move into this house to take care of your dad. Bill's raging anger only got worse when he got sick," Susan said, and then she hesitated just long enough for Alex to catch on.

"Were his outbursts about me?"

"You don't even need to ask, do you? Of course they were. To be honest, Annie never came out and defended you, but she did refuse to send the boys' gifts back to you when The Coach demanded it—it took a lot to stand her ground with that, believe it or not.

"She'll come around eventually—once she's had time to separate her beliefs from your father's. Many people were blind to Bill's unbalanced legalism." Susan motioned toward a group of men that included Jett.

"Jett's just like him," Alex blurted out.

"No, Alex, Jett is really a kind man. Kindness left your father decades ago, and I can't figure out why. I'm a conservative Christian, but not like Bill—he did great harm to the cause of Christ in all areas. I've even heard him make fun of Tom Hamilton. In this town there's not a more godly man than Harley's father."

"Tom Hamilton? The Coach was scared of him, that's all. He'd victimize people he was scared of," Alex replied.

"Scared of Tom Hamilton? Why?" Susan was curious.

"Why not? Tom is the better man and The Coach knew it. He had to win at everything. By picking on Tom—well, you understand, it made The Coach look good, or so he thought. What I can't understand is how you see it and they don't. The Coach turned Annie and her family against me," Alex said.

"When Bill had authority over a person he abused it. As far as Annie goes, she's Wayne's wife and I'm confident that Wayne's level-headedness will override Annie's emotional pull to continue to please Bill." She patted Alex's arm. *"Trust me on this. Annie will be there for you if you ever need her."*

"I'd like to believe that," he said to Susan.

In his hospital bed Alex repeated, *"I'd like to believe that."*

He still could see Annie as they put away the leftover food after the wake.

"I was glad to see Susan Spencer," Alex said, as he wrapped the food.

"She plans to retire next year, so I'll become chairman of the English department."

"Susan leaves you very big shoes to fill," Alex said.

Annie laughed. *"Yeah, it's like trying to wear Bozo's slippers."*

Being alone with Annie was not as difficult as he had anticipated. Alex wanted to talk with her like he had talked to Susan, but maybe it would come before the end of the evening.

"Susan plans to take life a little slower. She doesn't know what the Lord has in store for her, but she might even plan a trip to Atlanta." Annie sounded weary.

Susan had not even hinted at this. His heart leapt; Susan would bring back good news about his life in Atlanta.

"But I told her ..." Her back was to Alex as she poked the last pie into the refrigerator.

"Did you tell her not to come because I'm some sort of deviant?"

Alex swung around from the sink and years of suppressed anger raced through his body.

"Don't say those things about yourself." Annie closed the refrigerator door and pressed her skirt down as she started assembling desserts on the counter.

"Why not say it, Annie? People have been saying it since I arrived. Haven't you seen the stares and heard the whispers? What's wrong with you that you can't see what people have done to me?"

"I'm tired of dancing around this subject." She slammed a cake down on the counter. "I can't believe the crazy ideas you have."

"Don't start on me, or I don't know what I'll say." Alex struck a cabinet with his fist.

"Don't start on you? You've brought yourself to complete ruin. You could get AIDS, for God's sake, and then this life-partner business. I never thought I'd hear my brother talk about being in a union with a man. It's blasphemy."

"So you think I'm going to hell?" Alex sneered.

Annie sat down and rested her hand on her forehead. "You're working pretty hard on it."

"Narrow thinking like yours is what sends people to hell, Annie." Alex started to pour himself water and then threw it into the sink. The glass shattered.

"What are you talking about?" Annie looked as if she wanted to take her fists and beat him.

"I lived my whole life with ridicule. The Coach treated me like dirt because I wasn't like his star players. All his clone athletes harassed me. Not once did you, your husband, or anyone else in this town offer to help. Scott loves me without condition: my shortcomings as well as my strengths. I do have strengths, you know."

"But do you have AIDS?" she asked without emotion.

"Get back on the subject, Mrs. Whitley. Face it, not one person ever stood up for me. I never had buddies. I never had an intimate talk with a guy until I

moved to Atlanta. *Gay life may not be easy, but it sure beats the hell out of isolation." His knees felt weak.*

"I can't separate your sin from you. Every time you do whatever you do, you mock your supposed faith in Jesus Christ. You're just short..."

"Short of what? Judgment? Are you waiting for the fire to come down and consume me like Sodom and Gomorrah? Judgment like AIDS? Listen, honey, if I get AIDS, it won't be because I've slept with one guy after another. No, it will be on the heads of the good people of this crappy little town because they weren't there when I needed them." Alex began to cry. "It will be on The Coach—dear old Dad—and on you and Wayne, because you've alienated me like someone with the plague. I might as well have AIDS."

His face was hot with tears. "I was hoping that I'd been wrong all these years and maybe I could come home. Boy, was I stupid. Unconditional love isn't in your vocabulary. I'll be out of your house tomorrow. As for my inheritance, I don't want anything that belonged to Bill Marshall."

The last time Alex saw her, Annie was crying and picking up the broken glass. He left before she got out of bed the next morning.

In his hospital bed Alex wondered if he should call her.

"Susan said if I ever needed Annie, she'd be there. Well, let's try it," he said as he began dialing Annie's phone number.

4

WHITLEY HOME, HALLTON

"DAD, YOU'LL NEVER GUESS who's called." The gangly, pre-teen boy ran to tell his father.

"Get your breath and tell me," Wayne said as he turned the gas off on the grill. If it was half as urgent as Ben sounded, then he would need to go inside.

"Uncle Alex," he said with a look of wonder on his face. While Alex was already in Atlanta when he was born, Ben knew this was an answer to prayer for his family.

"You don't say," Wayne said as he headed up the steps into the kitchen. Once inside he could see that the conversation had obviously taken a grave turn. Annie was sinking down into the sofa. Her breathing was interspersed with moans that wanted to be something else, like a cry. Wayne shot a look at Brian, their seventeen-year-old son, who shrugged his shoulders. Apparently no one knew what Alex had just said to Annie.

"Sure, I think I can make it. I'll have to talk with Wayne first, but . . ." She nodded as if Alex was in the room. "Graduation is Friday, so I could leave Saturday or Sunday, or sooner . . . okay . . . okay. Let me have your number and I'll call you tomorrow evening."

Annie reached for a pad next to the telephone. Her hand shook so violently that Wayne had to steady it as he handed her a pen. He didn't need to ask anything, but he knew what he would hear once Annie hung up. He motioned for his sons to come into the kitchen. They were quick to respond.

"Brian, take Ben and get something to eat." Wayne handed him some cash. "Mom and I need to have time. No one needs to know Alex called. Understand?"

Wayne faced the most decisive moment of his life. He wished he had moved on it before now. Once the boys were gone, he sat down by Annie on the sofa to determine their next step.

A slight cry came from her lips after Annie put down the phone, but it was several minutes before she could utter a word. She looked around the room as if this was the last time she would see it. Her chin quivered.

"AIDS?" Wayne broke the silence.

Annie nodded as she wiped the tears.

"I can't believe it." She labored not to scream. "Alex is dying and said he needs me to help him at home. He says Stan—uh, Todd, no—Scott, yeah, Scott can't handle it by himself."

"You should go." Wayne took Annie's hand in his large rugged hand. "It's time we met Alex halfway."

Irritation flared in Annie's voice. "After what he's been doing? Just go to Atlanta and be a part of what he does?"

Wayne took her other hand and looked into her eyes. "Listen to what you're saying. Your dying brother has asked you to come to him. We'll never have another opportunity with him if you refuse this last request."

"He lives with a man as you and I live as husband and wife. We've been taught to not fellowship with someone who's in deliberate sin."

Annie did not want to do anything against scripture. She had held to the hope that her separation from Alex would make him aware of where sin had taken him. For years Annie had expected his return—she knew how much Alex cared for her and her family.

"In our zealousness, we've missed the basic truth of the Gospel. Sweetheart, I've—we've been broken over the situation with Alex, and we can't miss this opportunity," Wayne said firmly.

"I'll be living in his home, and that's condoning homosexuality."

"You may feel uncomfortable, but you must do it for Alex. It's been *five* years. You have no choice but to go."

Annie began pacing. "But shouldn't we show a solid front against sin to our sons?"

"Show them a woman who'll lay down her life for her brother. The decision is yours, but we're in Alex's final days."

Annie stood still. "What will you and the kids do?"

"We'll get by. Brian can take Ben to his ball games. We've got good neighbors who can help with any extra meals. Actually, I'm pretty handy in the kitchen in a pinch."

"The neighbors will talk." Annie began pacing again.

"Let them talk."

Annie calmed for a moment and then said pleadingly, "But I *can't* go into that gay atmosphere. I can only imagine what happens at their home."

"With a sick man? Forget it. You get things lined up at school, and I'll book your flight. Annie, once Alex dies there's no way to go back and correct the things we didn't do right. We'll talk to Clark—a pastor's blessing is important."

"What about Jett? He's experienced enough to counsel us."

"He's hardheaded like your father. Jett can't be objective—he never liked Alex."

"Jett never buckled under The Coach's authority," Annie declared. "Alex was a Christian man one day and the next he was gay? Why couldn't Alex have trusted Jesus more?" Annie shook her head.

"Why didn't we help him more?" Wayne got up to look for a phone book. "I'm booking your flight. We can't ignore the last chance the Lord has given us."

"You didn't answer me. Why couldn't Alex have trusted Jesus more?"

"I can't say, babe. Maybe you'll get your answer in Atlanta."

AUSTIN FIRST CHURCH ~ SUNDAY NIGHT

"We'll miss you, pastor. God bless you on your work," a college student said to him from across the aisle.

Samuel Phillips greeted each person who desired to shake his hand after the service. His plain-clothes bodyguards had stepped aside to let the people get close. Tonight he wanted to reach out to his congregation, and more than ever he needed to know people cared.

"Dr. Phillips, I've been here for many years. When you talked about your failures, I couldn't see them. You're quite a success, as far as I'm concerned," said Cindy Gregory, a longtime member. "We're so blessed to have a man who listens to God."

"Thank you, Cindy. I appreciate your faith in me, but as any man, I'm not perfect."

He became disgusted with himself as he heard his cliché words. Samuel felt like a spiritual fraud. His struggles were presented as victories won by having enough faith. The extent of his "faith" in the last two decades had been to control circumstances so they ensured the perfect outcome—faith had taken on less and less a role in his life as he became more successful.

Cindy walked toward the front doors, and Samuel turned to see the thinning crowd in the auditorium. It was mostly made up of people he had known for many years.

Denny Lawrence, head of the ushers, stood at the end of the aisle. He constantly battled lust. Tonight Samuel could see the hurt in Denny's wife, Helen. Months ago Samuel had given Denny a list of scriptures to hold on to and suggested that Helen be more submissive.

Talking with Helen was Candace Cooley. Candace had an abusive husband. Samuel had told her to stay in her marriage no matter what: "abuse" did not fall under the category of "adultery"—the only biblical reason to divorce.

"Your sermon had a good message, Samuel, but what was that comment about failing your congregation?" It was Gerald Eubanks. "You've always been too hard on yourself. This church has grown from a handful of members to more than fifteen thousand."

Samuel waved off his bodyguards and walked toward his office, speaking quietly to Eubanks.

"I appreciate your confidence. Losing Natalie—well, it changed the way I look at things. I've been reevaluating my priorities, and I feel a need to—uh—reconcile—um—things with people before it's too late."

"Samuel, if this is about Scott, we've been over this many times already," Eubanks interjected. "You did the right thing—you can't wink at sin."

As Eubanks continued to talk, Samuel noticed Candace and her daughters enter the hallway. He acknowledged her with a nod as she walked past and left the building. Was he imagining it, or did he see bruises on the children, also? Samuel knew he'd been wrong to tell Candace to stay in that dangerous environment.

"Right now I need to take care of some business, Gerald. Drop by for lunch one day this week." Samuel flashed a smile.

After talking with a few more people, Samuel slipped out to his car and went back to the cemetery. Speaking to his wife in the darkness, he was reminded of Nicodemus stealing away to speak with Jesus. For years he had been a Pharisee: a self-righteous person given to rules, tradition, and doctrine. Tonight the things he was considering weren't in line with the traditional spiritual beliefs of his church. Somehow, though, Samuel knew they were from God.

"Natalie, there's a woman in the church who's being hit and hurt. What should I do? If I were a regular man I'd take whatever steps necessary to make sure she was safe, but I'm not just any man. I answer to the church leadership—but these are godly men. Certainly they would help . . ."

Samuel sat on the tombstone, and after a long pause he continued. "Maybe they wouldn't. However, I think God wants me to help her. Everyone will think I've lost my mind because this could break up her home."

Again he stopped as if he was waiting for Natalie to respond.

"Once when you were angry at me about Scott, you told me that all I cared about was what other men thought." Samuel hesitated. "You were right, Nat."

Samuel looked up into the sky and wondered if he could ever do enough to be exonerated for his sins.

"I've been an absolute failure with my family, God. I don't blame Scott for hating me. If he knew about his mother . . ." Samuel stopped and patted the tombstone. "Natalie told me, God, I was too stubborn to truly pay attention to you."

Samuel listened to the crickets, looked at the stars, and felt the warm, ever-present breeze on his face.

"God, I'm ready to listen. Just show me where to begin."

5

HALLTON⁀MONDAY, MAY 30

"Jett phoned to say he'll be a few minutes late," Pastor Clark Perkins said.

Annie and Wayne sat on the sofa in his office. Annie was too distraught to speak.

"No problem. I'll tell you about Alex while we wait," Wayne began. "Jett knows everything that's happened."

"Please go ahead—why don't you just give a little family background. I only know of The Coach through Jett quoting him all the time," Clark said. He had become the church's pastor the summer after The Coach's death. A man in his late fifties, Clark had a reputation for standing with families through thick and thin.

"Laura—Annie and Alex's mom—was a real sweet girl," began Wayne. "She and Bill married when they were in their mid-twenties—Laura was already pregnant with Annie. There was gossip that The Coach was still sowing his wild oats. Laura apparently knew about it—at least she believed the rumors—and in order to cope she began drinking." Wayne was about to continue when Clark interrupted him.

"He wasn't a Christian at this time?"

"Heavens no, that happened after Laura died. The Coach focused all his attention on being the biggest name in Wisconsin high school football and trying to make Alex his hero athlete son. When Alex failed to meet The Coach's expectations, and that was often, The Coach took it out on him. It was almost like he thought Alex wasn't trying on purpose. Laura stopped being social."

"How did he 'take it out on Alex'?" Clark asked.

"The Coach thought corporal punishment was the only way to teach anyone anything. Alex always got more than his share." Wayne shook his head with the memory.

"I can remember Mom trying to stop him at first, but with things like that, he didn't want her input," Annie said. "When he was busy during football season, she was much more outgoing. But by the time I was in second grade, she was self-medicated most of the time."

"There is a great deal of mystery to Laura's life. Once she died the way she did, and The Coach had failed as a husband—I think it made him start thinking about changing his image. That's when he became a Christian, at least outwardly."

"How did he treat you, Annie?" Clark asked.

"About like everyone else, but I conformed to what he wanted," Annie said matter-of-factly.

"Did your mom commit suicide? I thought I heard that somewhere. It might have been from you, Annie," Clark said.

Annie was in deep thought, and when she didn't respond to Clark's question, Wayne decided to answer.

"It wasn't intentional. It's always been my belief that she was trying to numb the pain of her life. Finally, one day, the combination of drugs and alcohol proved fatal."

Wayne quietly pondered his next statement.

"The Coach took on a sort of zealousness about his Christianity. He began to have rigidity about life, and he was continually finger-pointing people's sins."

"Did he do it to you or Alex?" Clark asked Annie.

"He just left us alone so he could be the hero out there in the community. Alex and I basically raised ourselves—that is unless we broke one of his household rules. When that happened we were punished," Annie said.

"The Coach was a spiritual leader to guys like Jett, but he and Alex were like oil and water," Wayne added. "I guess over the years Alex could only take so much."

"When did he leave?" Clark asked.

"Late summer of 1981," Wayne answered. "Alex had lived in Green Bay since he first went to college. He told his roommates he was going to Atlanta on business. The Coach didn't question it because he'd only see Alex on holidays. By that time they were cordial, but not much more—if he was in Hallton for more than a meal, Alex spent the time down at our house."

"How did you find out that Alex was gay?" Clark asked.

"How did we find out?" Wayne looked at Annie.

Her voice was weak and hoarse. "Alex had been gone for almost a year. Ben was a couple of months old, and Alex sent some gifts. He included a letter telling me he was starting law school, and he was gay.

"Alex used to be so dedicated to Jesus. After college he fulfilled his life-long dream of joining Community Challenge for Christ. When we got the letter, Wayne and I went to Green Bay to talk with the two guys he'd roomed with, and they were shocked.

"I never allowed myself to believe he was gay until The Coach's funeral. When Alex got off the plane I could see the change. I was mortified and kept my distance. Clark, how could this have happened?" Annie rested her head against the sofa and closed her eyes.

"After he wrote you, do you think you'd have included Alex in your life had The Coach not been around?" Clark inquired.

"We can look back and say that we might have tried to reconcile our relationship, but in reality I think we'd have done things pretty much the way we did them. It seemed right at the time. Even now we don't want to accept his life or his friend, but Alex is dying and he wants to make peace."

Clark absorbed Wayne's statement. "Let's backtrack a little. Do you have any idea why Alex felt he had to leave so suddenly?"

"No one knows what triggered it," Wayne said as he put his arm around Annie. "It must have been a collection of things over the years, even though it appeared to happen without warning."

"Unquestionably, Alex's earthly example of God—his father—thought Alex was less than a man. It's my opinion that Annie must go to Atlanta."

"Atlanta?" Jett asked as he entered the room. "Are you going to see Alex?"

Jett was six-foot-two and still muscular from his football days. The only change was wire-rimmed glasses that complemented his broad round features, curly brown hair, and gentle blue-green eyes. He was wearing khaki shorts and a white shirt. The color in his cheeks told them he had been golfing. Jett shook Wayne's hand and then hugged Annie.

"Wayne, would you brief Jett?" Clark requested.

"Alex has AIDS. He called yesterday asking Annie to come take care of him once he gets out of the hospital. Annie and I desire your blessing on this journey."

"I'm so sorry, Annie. When it happens you're never ready. I must say I've expected to hear this for quite some time." Jett sat down beside her.

"I believe God can use Annie to get through to Alex, although his time is short," Clark began.

"I'd like to warn them of some things," Jett interrupted. "Homosexuality is a deadly sin. These men have made a mockery of the sanctity of marriage. Alex has no plan to return to Jesus. Annie, once you get there I'm afraid your concern for Alex will outweigh your discernment. Before you know it you'll be ensnared in their hotbed of sin and begin accepting things you should be speaking against."

His sincerity sent chills down Annie's spine.

"You know I love your family and felt that your father was my own. Have you considered telling Alex that you won't come unless he recommits his life to the Lord?"

"Jett, I disagree," Clark said, in a firm voice. "When Annie takes the love of Jesus into the *hotbed of sin* it will show Alex unconditional love, the kind of love Jesus teaches us to give. Wayne and Annie's approach has more of a chance of succeeding than yours."

"The Coach always said Alex needed a firm hand," Jett persisted. "Once Alex's health improves will you invite the lover boy up here on holidays? I mean, this can get complicated if you aren't careful. What about the boys? You'll be putting them at risk."

"Alex would never hurt our sons. Otherwise, you have made a good argument, but that isn't what God is telling us. Our minds are made up," Wayne said.

Annie gulped and looked down at her lap. Jett took advantage of Annie's pause and grabbed her hand.

"Annie agrees with me. This has been a nightmare, because all these years Alex has only thought of himself." Jett looked up at the men and finished. "Now his sin has brought him full circle. The scripture says the wages of sin is death, and Alex is dying because of his sin."

Wayne took Annie's hand from Jett. He was bothered by Jett's response.

"As much as The Coach did for you, I thought you'd be more support-ive," Wayne said. "We don't need your blessing. What you say might be rele-vant for another situation, but it's not how God is moving us. Somehow we must show the love of Jesus to Alex and Scott—that's the boyfriend—without crossing the biblical boundaries."

Jett's hands opened wide as if he had dropped a large object. "That's a wonderful concept, but how can it be accomplished? It's impossible to see Alex without compromising the Gospel."

"We'll follow what the Bible truly teaches: unconditional love, grace, mercy, forgiveness, for starts. This is our last chance with Alex," Wayne said. He and Annie got up from the sofa. "Gentlemen, we need to let you have the rest of your Memorial Day with your families."

The Whitleys left the room as Jett sat shaking his head.

"What is it? What really bothers you about Annie going to Atlanta?" Clark asked.

"To start, she's being drawn into a deceptive environment. Alex and his friend could prove to be a serious problem in terms of safety for her boys. Not to mention Brian and Ben might come to think this lifestyle is accept-able and want to embrace it for themselves. I know Annie can handle the Atlanta situation, but where will it end? Every day we see people fooled by sin."

Clark studied Jett. The irritation he felt toward Jett came frequently these days. This youth pastor was growing rigid on matters of the Gospel. Clark couldn't understand because Jett was otherwise compassionate.

"Were you ever jealous of Alex?"

"Never."

"That answer was certainly emphatic—are you sure?" Clark continued to look closely at Jett's eyes.

"No, Clark, I didn't like him because he ruined his father's good name—that's all," Jett replied.

"Well, I hope Annie proves you wrong," Clark said. "Jett, if Jesus were here today, what would he do?"

"I don't think he'd go see Alex." Jett walked back to the desk and picked up his Bible. "Shouldn't Alex be held accountable for his sins? I grew up with The Coach, too, and I never made excuses."

"Have some mercy, Jett; people are different," Clark said as Jett joined him at the door. "At least support them through prayer. You can do that, can't you? Stretch your faith and maybe God will be able to use you. Go home and enjoy your family. It's Memorial Day."

Jett stood silently next to the bench outside the office as Clark disappeared around the corner. That night in Green Bay flashed into his mind. He shook his head to clear his memory and his Bible fell to the floor. On top of the scattered papers was a brochure from a pro-life rally. Jett picked it up and sat down on the bench.

"How could Alex have known about Rita and me . . . and the baby? *No one knew*—not even Harley," Jett said quietly to himself as he looked at the brochure.

Today was the first time in years he had thought of that night and the terrible days that followed. It had been a boil on his soul for years, and now Annie was going to see Alex.

Jett picked up his papers and then tested the doorknob to Clark's office to make sure it was locked. On his way out to the car he thought: *Well, it could be worse. Alex could be coming to Hallton.*

PART TWO

❧ The Trip ❧

I am so weak that I can hardly write, I cannot read my Bible, I cannot even pray, I can only lie still in God's arms like a little child, and trust.

Hudson Taylor

6

HARTSFIELD INTERNATIONAL AIRPORT, ATLANTA—WEDNESDAY, JUNE 1

SCOTT JIGGLED HIS KEYS as he watched Annie at the luggage bin. She was pretty, with the same hair color and casual demeanor as Alex. As they talked coming from the deplaning area, Annie used her hands expressively just like Alex. Scott was nervous about feeling so familiar with her—it might cause him to let down his guard.

In no time they were in the parking lot walking through the blanket of heat to his Jeep.

"Wow, I always heard about the humidity in Georgia, but never could I have imagined this," Annie remarked.

"It was hard for me to get used to," Scott said.

"Where are you from?" Annie asked.

She observed Scott as she kept up with his quick pace. Annie expected him to be the type of gay man she had seen on television—loud, effusive, and effeminate. However, Scott had no prissy movements or affected speech. His blond hair tossed about in the breeze. Annie knew when she wrote in her journal she would describe Scott as irresistibly handsome. He was rugged, like Robert Redford with a day's beard growth.

"The Southwest—oh, look, we're here," Scott said as he pointed to his vehicle.

Scott opened her door and then put her bags in the rear. Soon he had the engine started and the air conditioner was cooling the interior. Before he left the parking space, he turned toward her to speak. Scott's expression was reassuring, but his voice was hesitant.

"Allow me to drive you past Alex's law office. When you see him it could be a topic of conversation," Scott said.

"Do you think we'll need one for some reason?" Annie was puzzled.

"Alex doesn't look like himself. He's been extremely worried that you'll be alarmed. This is a way to get around the shock," Scott said. He wanted to prepare her as much as he could.

"That's very kind of you. Yes, I think maybe we ought to do that," Annie replied.

As they headed toward the interstate, Scott began telling her about Alex's accomplishments over the last ten years. Annie was impressed. Alex had enjoyed professional success as well as community-wide respect.

It wasn't long before they were moving slowly through the downtown Atlanta traffic. Annie's eyes scanned the multilevel tower where Alex's office was located. He hadn't practiced law for almost a year.

"How is Alex taking being labeled as disabled?" she asked.

"The partners call him once or twice a week for his opinion. Everyone is pitching in to keep Alex encouraged so he'll continue to fight. Down deep he knows he isn't going back. He has an excellent disability policy. Basically, we're set financially."

Annie had been having a pleasant time so far, but hearing Scott say "we" and knowing he was talking about another man and that man was her brother stiffened Annie right up. All the warm feelings immediately vanished. Homosexuality had a bitter taste, and the sooner her visit to Atlanta was over, the better.

"Are you an attorney also?" Annie inquired in an effort to change the subject.

"No, I own a newspaper for the gay community. I started it when I was in college."

"I see. Well, it seems you're very industrious. I'd like to read it sometime." In truth, Annie had no desire to read such trash.

"Sure. I can get a copy for you. I hope you won't be bored while you're here. Alex and I are pretty much homebodies."

Annie sucked in air and then slowly let it out hoping Scott wouldn't see her disgust.

"If I've offended you, I'm truly sorry."

"No, no. You're talking about a man who's almost middle age," Annie said to cover. "I've had so little contact with Alex that it's hard to imagine him much beyond his college years."

Scott collected his thoughts. "Annie, the doctor has instructed the staff to give him a mild sedative so the impact of seeing you won't ..." Scott swallowed hard.

"Please, go on."

Annie noticed that Scott was fighting tears, but she was at a loss. This wasn't in the *How to Be a Christian* handbook. Scott was genuinely kind, but he was also her brother's lover. As she struggled internally, Scott pulled into the driveway. After the automobile was in park, he looked at her with a new intensity.

"Sometimes if he gets too excited his breathing becomes affected or he starts coughing or throwing up. I want him to be well enough to have time with you," Scott said sincerely.

"Thank you for inviting me," Annie replied.

Annie looked at the house that her brother called home. She would never accept Alex's lifestyle, but she wanted to make peace with him and his friend Scott.

"Let's put your bags in the house, and then we'll be off to the hospital." Scott got her suitcase and walked in the back gate toward the house.

ᑯ ᑯ ᑯ

"Third floor, room 317. We'll take this corridor," Scott instructed, as they walked down the gray carpet. Scott tried to encourage Annie. "We take this one moment at a time. Okay? Here's his room."

The massive door to room 317 was cracked two inches, and the overwhelming smell of bleach coming from within permeated Annie's sinuses instantly. Her eyes filled with tears and her heart raced.

"Just a minute," Annie said. She grabbed Scott's arm. He was the only one who could help her with her complex feelings: fear, anxiety, and regret. Annie breathed deeply and fanned her face.

"Are you okay?" Scott held her shoulders to keep her from fainting. "He's excited to see you—think about only that. I'll go in first and you watch from the door."

Scott found Alex napping. He took his frail arm and gently shook it. Scott then bent and whispered something to him. Leaning against the wall, Annie prayed, and then she took a deep breath and walked into the room. The thin sheets shook as Alex's body quaked with emotion when he saw Annie.

All the books she had read and the photographs Scott had shown her did not prepare Annie for the reality of AIDS. Only the pictures she'd seen of concentration camp survivors compared to how frail, bony, and weak Alex looked. The spots on his yellow skin made him look as though he had been beaten with a small hammer. Everything about him signified death.

"Alex, I'm here," she said as she walked up beside the bed. The frail man bore little resemblance to her brother. Annie could hardly contain her tears as she embraced him. How could something like this happen to a human?

"Annie," Alex said just before he began gasping for breath. He motioned for Scott to buzz a nurse. It was less than a minute before one was in the room giving Alex more oxygen and a small pill.

Scott mouthed to Annie, "To sleep."

Annie held Alex's hand as his breathing steadied. She wondered if Alex would die right then. There would be no time for apologies, no time to get reacquainted, and no time to talk to him about Jesus. Now Annie knew she had to muster whatever internal resources were necessary to be there for Alex until the end.

Alex was almost asleep when Scott bent over the bed rail and whispered to him. "I'm taking Annie for a hospital tour. You rest and we'll be back in a while."

Scott motioned to Annie. Once they were in the hall Annie began to cry. "We're close to the end." Scott gave her his handkerchief. He looked at her with compassion and then added, "I'm glad you could come."

Annie nodded as she wiped her eyes. Without another word they walked down the hall.

AUSTIN↝WEDNESDAY EVENING

Samuel Phillips sat on his velvet-covered altar chair and looked over the congregation. Everything tonight was uncomfortable: his suit, shirt, tie, and the chair. His church had a reputation as one where you could come meet Jesus, and thousands had come for that experience. Along the way, Samuel knew he had missed something that was vitally important. The "something" wasn't a complete concept, just a queasy feeling within his soul.

What has held me back? He knew it had to be what kept him from doing the things he needed to do for Candace and others like her, as well as what kept him from contacting Scott.

At that moment Candace came through the double doors wearing sunglasses. She glided into the seat next to Mayzelle Eubanks. Her two girls huddled close to her. Brent was rarely with them. As with everything he always had an excuse.

Why aren't the girls in their Wednesday evening program? Samuel wondered.

A minute into the night's songs Samuel looked at Candace again. She had not taken off her sunglasses and her hair covered her face. A sick feeling went through him.

For years Brent had blamed Candace for his anger. Samuel had perpetuated Brent's denial by telling Candace to follow 1 Peter 3:1. That verse was considered a prescription from God on how to change a husband who was not being the Christian he needed to be. All a wife needed to do was be submissive, maintain godly behavior, and, according to the scripture, the man would see his error and transform.

God hates divorce, but I can't let Candace be brutalized . . . Enough is enough.

Samuel was glad he was not leading the Bible study tonight. All he could do was feign interest as the associate pastor began speaking. The thought kept returning: *How could it be biblical to pull Candace out of her home—could it keep them from divorce? Or push them straight into court?*

Samuel's secretary, Esther, was in the front row pew. She might know where Candace and the girls could go. They needed someone to intervene on their behalf. Samuel heard the associate pastor say, "In these verses husbands are told to love their wives with the same love that Christ showed the church."

Suddenly he had a plan. Samuel jotted a message and motioned for Esther to meet him at the altar. It was common for him to ask her for a book or notes during a service. No one thought anything about it when he handed the piece of paper to Esther that read: *Find C. Cooley after service. Bring to my office. Need to find a safe place.* Esther smiled and nodded. Maybe helping Candace was the beginning of finding the answer to the questions that harassed his soul.

e~ e~ e~

Later that evening, Samuel knocked at the front door to the Cooley home. After a few minutes a man opened the door. Brent appeared to have been sleeping.

"Brother Samuel, what a surprise to see you." His tone became serious. "Do you know if everything is okay with Candace? She's not home and I've been worried sick."

Samuel had a hard time restraining himself from punching him. When Candace had taken off her sunglasses in his office she looked worse than Phillips had imagined. The children were shell-shocked.

"She's in a safe place," Samuel said. "May I come in and talk?"

Brent stepped back for him to step inside the foyer. The house was perfectly in order—except that Samuel could see that around Brent's leather chair was a mass of newspapers, food trays, empty chip sacks, and soda bottles. Brent clicked off the television, and then it registered with him what Samuel had said.

"Hey, what's this 'safe place' business?"

"You heard me. Tonight Candace came to church looking like a punching bag. My secretary has taken your family to a domestic violence shelter where they'll be safe."

❧ 34 ☙

"You know how clumsy Candace is. She fell."

Samuel put up his arm with an opened hand like a policeman stopping a car. "No more lies. You have a problem. It's time you face up to that. Your wife won't be the outlet for your rage any longer."

"What are you accusing me of? I've approved loans for the church. I've required no collateral or down payment when—" Brent started before he was interrupted.

"You always know how to get the focus off yourself, don't you, Brent? I'm tired of your threats. Any bank in this town would like to have our account," Samuel said. "You can no longer ignore what you've been doing to your family."

"You're a dirty old man who's in love with my wife. What sort of lies are you starting about me?" Brent shouted.

"I'm here to offer you my time to help you make your marriage work. I'll go with you to whatever group you need to attend," Samuel said calmly. "I'll pay for the counseling sessions if you don't want it to appear on your insurance. The bottom line is that you must address the root of your violent nature. Understand?"

"Get out of my house. I understand I've got a preacher in my house that's walking outside the Word of God. My wife has to submit to me." Brent came toward Samuel, pointing his finger at him. "You've caused her to have a Jezebel spirit by coddling her in her lack of submission to my authority."

Brent reached out to punch Samuel, but Samuel grabbed Brent's arm with little effort. Clearly surprised, Brent knew the older man had beaten him.

"Stop your shouting, Brent." Samuel was still calm, but firm. "Yes, in Ephesians 5 the Lord says for wives to submit to their husbands. As well in Ephesians—so we're talking about the same author—it says to be truthful and not let your anger grow into a sin. By hitting Candace you haven't loved your wife as Christ loved the church. Did Jesus ever hit *anyone*? The answer is no, and you know it. Brent, you've taken your anger to a sinful level. As well, you haven't been truthful about your problem—not eight years ago and not even tonight. You *must* get help. If you like we'll go to another town where we're not known. While I'm in Peru, Gerald Eubanks can go with you. He's a trustworthy man."

"Get out of my house!" Brent shouted again. "I'll show you! No one is going to take my family away from me."

As he stepped outside the door, Samuel stopped. "You're right. No one has taken your family from you. You've managed to do it all by yourself."

Brent slammed the door with such force that Samuel could feel the wind. He was glad he had helped Candace, and tonight getting her out of harm's way was more important than the ultimate consequences. Samuel felt like his teenaged self back when he gave his life to the Lord and had a big future ahead of him. That feeling told Samuel he was on the right track.

7

HALLTON · THURSDAY, JUNE 2

Many mornings Jett would stop by just to say hello to Harley. It was great having him home from prison, where he had served almost four years for gambling on his own professional games and drug possession. This visit, however, wasn't so much to encourage his old friend as to inquire about something from years ago.

Since the meeting with Annie and Wayne, God had been dealing with Jett. He felt compelled to confess his secret to someone, but revealing it would expose him as a hypocrite. The only person Jett could trust to still care about him, once the truth came to light, was Harley.

Jett pulled into the driveway of the sprawling white farmhouse. It was early, but Harley had apparently already been working in the barn for hours. He was covered with dirt and perspiration. When he saw Jett, a wide grin crossed his face.

"Come help me put down straw," Harley hollered.

"Can't—I'm dressed for work," Jett shouted back as he got out of his car.

Harley took off his work gloves and motioned for Jett to come sit with him in the chairs under the shade of the trees.

"Why are you up so early? Nightmares again?" Jett asked.

Harley nodded. Since he had been released in February, Harley had had recurring nightmares of breaking the law again.

"I decided to be productive and get started on cleaning the horse stalls," he replied.

"When do you think you all can come over for dinner? Donna wanted me to check." Jett was losing his nerve to confess.

"I'll confirm with Kitty, but I think next week would be good," Harley said as he grabbed a stick to get a clump of mud off his boot.

"I've been thinking about some of the things we talked about over the last few years." Jett proceeded carefully to not give himself away. "I guess I never asked, but I was just wondering if you ever got anyone pregnant?"

He instantly felt guilty about putting his friend on the spot—asking Harley to reveal the very thing he himself wanted to keep secret.

"Wow, I didn't see that one coming," Harley said.

"Um, well, maybe we just need to forget it," Jett said hurriedly, drawing his arms back to push himself up from the chair.

Harley gently reached over and put his hand on Jett's shoulder.

"Years ago Kitty said she didn't want to know, but since I became a Christian I've been very honest with her about everything down to the last loan shark, hooker, and addiction. It's just strange you asked because it's been on my mind, wondering whether I should be honest with her about this, too."

"So you have?" Jett asked.

Harley pulled a cigarette out of a pack lying on the table and lit it before he continued talking. "Yes."

"Really? I sort of figured, I guess, because of the number of girls through the years," Jett said nervously.

"I was always cautious. I liked this girl, and she stayed around long enough for me to get careless."

"What did you do?" Jett thought his beating heart would jump out of his chest. It took everything within him not to confess at this moment.

"When she told me I pulled $500 out of my wallet and told her to get rid of it. Said I didn't need a baby ruining my life. I left and never called again. It was the most despicable thing I've ever done to anyone." Harley didn't make eye contact.

Harley took another puff and then held up the cigarette for Jett to see. "You know I'm working on giving these up—started this habit in prison. I can't run like I used to anymore. I figure I'll get lung cancer if I don't tell Kitty pretty soon. I've been chain-smoking since I started thinking about it." Harley then looked at Jett quizzically. "Did God prompt you to ask me?"

"You can say that," Jett replied, trying to keep his composure. Immediately he felt the Lord's conviction pushing him to make his own confession. Instead he hedged once again.

"Anyway, to answer your question: I've carried a pang of guilt ever since. As a way to make amends, I did write the girl a note of apology last year. She never replied, and I guess that was for the best," Harley said.

"Why didn't you tell me?" Jett asked.

"Right after it happened—I mean within a week—I was arrested on the gambling charge. As time went by and God started dealing with me, I was simply too ashamed."

"I admire you for being honest." Jett was genuine with his words.

Harley looked squarely at Jett, sensing he was troubled.

"Well, if you ever want to tell me about your deep sins—like the time you forgot to put your blinker on when changing lanes—let me know." Harley smiled. "You know, you could put on some work clothes and help me work on the roof before the storm rolls in today."

Jett wished he could, but he needed to get on the road. As he got into the car, Jett knew he was running from God's attempt to make him correct the past. But Jett was pretty sure that once Alex Marshall died this feeling would go away. Then he would never have to think about it again.

8

FRIDAY, JUNE 3, 3:30 A.M.

ANNIE HELD ONTO THE SINK to keep from dropping from exhaustion. The doctor was right—Scott needed all the help when Alex was back at home. If Alex didn't improve soon they would need another person to help on a full-time basis.

Early in the afternoon they brought Alex to the house. He was doing well when they left the hospital, but things changed quickly. The normally short trip took an hour because of how sick Alex became with the motion of the car. Scott carried Alex inside, and by the time they got to the bedroom his suit was covered with a slimy vomit that smelled of rotting sickness.

The home health nurse, Sharon Robbins, was in the driveway when they arrived. She returned to the Marshall-Phillips home twice more that day. Each time she encouraged Annie and Scott to not worry. She expected Alex to improve within the next twenty-four hours.

"Scott has gone to the pharmacy to get an inhalant that will help Alex's breathing," Sharon said as she packed her medical bag. "I've given Alex a sedative that should give you and Scott several hours to rest."

"How can you do this day after day?" Annie rubbed her eyes. "I'd never get used to this horrid illness."

"Horrid is an understatement."

"Aren't you afraid? Why do you risk your life?" Annie asked.

In Hallton life was a well-oiled machine. Her faith was never challenged like it had been since she arrived in Atlanta. Annie wondered how Jett would fare if he had a family member with this disease.

"I'm careful, and believe that God will take care of the circumstances." Sharon grabbed a sandwich from the full tray that one of Scott's friends had dropped off earlier. "My husband and I both work for an agency that specializes in home health care for AIDS patients. May I have a cup of black coffee to go with my sandwich?"

"Of course." Annie poured the coffee while she continued talking. "So you're a Christian? Where I live Christians don't align themselves with this disease."

"It's the same here. People who don't know better put the blame on the victims." Sharon took the cup from Annie's hand. "Some people call AIDS a curse for homosexuality. If that were true lesbians would be dying as fast as gay men. I've never treated more than a couple of lesbians in all the years I've worked with AIDS. I think it's an affliction on the generation who bought the lie of casual sex."

Annie shook her head. "But these men who have AIDS have led a promiscuous life."

"Annie, people in heterosexual relationships have it, too. The only difference is the gay community has a support system," Sharon asserted.

"Gay people help more than other people?" Annie sounded skeptical, but she was open to what Sharon's experience could teach her.

"Outside the gay community people stigmatize the person who's dying of AIDS as well as their family. When it comes to a person as sick as Alex, does it really matter how he got it? Imagine having no help. I've cooked food, emptied garbage, and washed dishes for straight people whose families have abandoned them.

"What would happen in your church if someone brought in a little girl with HIV? Would she get invited to a birthday party? Would she be able to participate in Sunday school? No way. One person with HIV can have the whole family banished from a town. How many times do born-again believers step in? Rarely—they'd rather ignore it. Consider Matthew 25."

"I can't remember what it says," Annie replied.

"It's about Jesus rewarding those who have served him. Roughly paraphrased: *I was thirsty, and you gave me a drink; I was a stranger, and you invited me in.* It goes on to talk about looking after the sick. Jesus told us to look after the sick, plain and simple. He didn't say anything about knowing where they got their illness. AIDS is a horrible way to die. I wish people would wake up and help people in need. It's a vast mission field for anyone who wants to serve God," Sharon said.

"But this lifestyle *isn't* normal," Annie pressed.

"When I'm at the bedside of someone who's dying, I'm nursing a human being. Someone whose basic needs are as important as yours, or those of your children," Sharon said. After a silent moment, she smiled and said, "I've got to run. By the end of the day you'll see an improvement in Alex. Trust me; you have plenty of time to spend with your brother."

Sharon rose from her chair, rinsed the coffee cup, and walked out the back door, past Scott who was returning from his pharmacy run. After a few minutes with Alex, Scott came back to the kitchen.

"How is he doing?" Annie sat down and sipped her cup of lukewarm coffee.

"The Pentamidine worked. Amazing what a $1,000 drug will do."

"You paid *$1,000* for *one* prescription?" Annie was astonished.

"When Alex took AZT our pharmacy bill ran to thousands of dollars a month, sometimes more depending on what was being tried at the time. If it extends his time, then it's worth every penny. Imagine all the people who aren't as lucky and don't have insurance."

"How *do* they afford treatment?" Annie asked.

"People do without and get sick quickly, or work it out with some mail-order pharmaceutical company to get on a payment plan. The real travesty is how few doctors will treat AIDS. In many areas of the United States there's only one doctor within one hundred miles who will treat an AIDS patient. I know of a doctor in rural Iowa who has three dozen patients. He has to come to the hospital on his off day to treat his patients—no other doctor will help. No one wants to risk exposing their other patients or themselves."

"I imagine in Hallton we'd have to travel to Green Bay, and someone in Alex's condition couldn't make that trip. That doesn't seem right at all."

For the first time Annie felt concern for people with AIDS. Until now it had been a gay disease.

Scott stood and stretched.

"I'm exhausted. I've forwarded the phone to the office answering service. If your family calls, the service will give them my cell number and I'll wake you." Scott hugged her. "Good night, thanks for all your help." He walked to Alex's room where he would sleep on a recliner.

Annie pondered her conversations with Scott and Sharon in the context of all she had been taught in church. She didn't have the answer she needed. Hopefully it would come soon.

9

FAMILY RESTAURANT, AUSTIN
THURSDAY, JUNE 9

"Samuel, the reason I've asked you to breakfast isn't social," Gerald Eubanks said sternly as he wiped coffee from his mouth. His bloated fingers clutched the white paper napkin.

"I figured that. So why didn't you just come down the hall and talk? You didn't have to make a special effort."

Eubanks always did this before he was about to reprimand someone. However, Samuel wasn't intimidated. Every day he was feeling more like he needed to go outside his comfort zone to help people. Eubanks would never understand.

"You're breaking up a marriage."

"Brent did that; I'm just saving the lives of his wife and children."

"I don't like your smug tone," Eubanks said. His brow was knitted with concern.

"Smug? No, it's simply that God doesn't want anyone to be abused," Samuel replied.

"Biblically you were wrong to take Candace from her husband." Eubanks pointed a finger in the pastor's face. "Brent Cooley wants you put out of the church. Unless you can give me a good reason why you did this, then I'll agree with him."

"Well, she sat next to you and your wife Wednesday evening with the bruises all over her face. Try that for starts."

"I didn't see any bruises," Eubanks protested.

"Do you think by ignoring it that this abuse will go away? This has been going on for years, and it's time for it to stop."

"You've gone off the deep end," Eubanks said angrily.

"Maybe I have, but I'm ready to do whatever it takes to save Candace's life and her marriage. I plan to invest time in Brent so he'll turn his life around. Christians must be in the business of meeting social challenges as well as spiritual ones. We've failed our people, Gerald."

"I see no failure," Eubanks said.

"I've ignored the needs of people in our church who are hurting. For years I advised Candace to be submissive, but Brent clearly wasn't doing his part as her husband.

"I've preached against mothers working outside the home. Yet there are many who must and I've placed unnecessary guilt on them. I want to take steps to correct that, too."

"A mother's place is in the home. The family must sacrifice." Eubanks accentuated each word to convey their importance.

"Sure, we have people in our church who love their possessions. On the other hand there are single mothers, or men who are unable to support their families. Instead of preaching condemnation, why haven't we set up affordable daycare with good help?"

"We'd be going against the Bible, Samuel. Have you've lost your mind?"

Samuel shook his head. Then he stopped, and it was obvious he was thinking. Suddenly Samuel was excitedly tapping his index finger on the table.

"Gerald, I have a great idea: if we forfeit our big television budget — I mean get rid of it completely—we could use that money for a daycare. I could spend part of my day there with the children. I'd like to see what we can get started by the fall."

"Spend your valuable time and sacrifice the television ministry for a group of children? Your sermons reach tens of thousands across America. You aren't making sense. There's more to this, isn't there, Samuel?"

"Yes." Samuel hesitated, knowing that Eubanks would give him a stern rebuke. He had to continue, because it was the right thing to do. "Recently I have wondered why I believed Chad Masters over my own son. Why did I just assume it was Scott who was the aggressor? In a few months we knew Chad had a problem. Gerald, Chad was a middle-aged man and Scott wasn't even eighteen! That's a crime."

"Don't kid yourself, Samuel. Scott was every bit as much to blame as Chad. What you need to do is pray for Scott's wretched soul to be saved from the fires of hell. You've done nothing wrong."

Eubanks looked pleased with himself as he took another sip of coffee.

"Honestly, at times recently I think you'd compromise your faith to get Scott back." Eubanks shook his head and muttered something unintelligible under his breath.

"Gerald, I compromised my faith the day I didn't run after him and repent for what I did to him. And it was wrong not telling him about his mother's cancer. What I'm doing for Candace is just one thing in the long list for me to be a good pastor."

"Candace leaving Brent isn't biblical. It's some sort of New Age, politically correct idea to keep a woman in rebellion."

Eubanks's mantra was commonly used by church figures to stop any independent thought that might challenge traditional, conservative methods. Samuel knew this ploy and continued.

"Well, if Brent hit *you*, would you sit there and let it happen over and over again?"

Eubanks shook his head. "Brent said he's working on his temper."

"He's been saying that for years, and it's only gotten worse. God doesn't want Candace and the girls to have to live in that environment. Brent needs help, and I've extended my support in every way. I've offered to pay for counseling and to go with him to his sessions."

"You did not. Brent hasn't mentioned that."

"And you believe him over me? I know it's more comfortable to avoid a conflict with our banker than to challenge him to be a biblical husband. But he's abusing his wife, and it's a sin."

"What if he doesn't change? Will you tell Candace to divorce? Even remarry?"

"It's up to Brent. You and I need to help him make the right choices. The first step was to hold him accountable for his deeds."

Eubanks ignored him.

"As I said, Brent has asked that we penalize you for your actions. I was asked to meet with you to get your side before we—"

"Dismiss me?" Samuel laughed because he knew that was where Eubanks was going with this conversation. "The irony of it all. Don't worry, Gerald, you have my resignation right now. I always said that if my elders didn't agree with my decisions, I'd resign. I'll make it official Sunday."

"You can't be serious." Eubanks flailed his hands.

"It's better than being responsible for Candace risking her life," Samuel replied. "I've made my choice. You've got my resignation. Now I must attend to my work."

"You're being deceived by the devil," Eubanks said loud enough for other people to hear.

"No I'm not—you are." Samuel stood up as people stared. "Thanks for breakfast, Gerald."

With that Samuel Phillips was off to the church. For the first time in weeks he could see the light at the end of the tunnel. There was one more thing he had to stop avoiding, something he had avoided for fifteen years.

THE PRIDE POSITION OFFICE, ATLANTA

"No, no, Annie is very sweet. Much to my surprise she isn't the 'Wicked Witch of the East.'"

Scott laughed with his executive staff as they sat around the conference table. He had been working since sunrise to complete the Gay Pride special edition issue before *The Pride Position* went to press at noon. Scott had been out of character by being so carefree.

"Actually, it's very livable. I can see Annie wince when Alex and I get close, but other than that she's been perfect." Scott smiled and then took another bite of omelet.

Lesley stopped proofing her editorial. "So how's Alex? I've been scared to ask."

"He's doing well. He can walk around a little." Scott sipped his iced tea. "A couple of people dropped by last night; now he claims he's ready for more company today."

"And you thought last week it was over," Lesley smiled. "How long will his sister be here?"

"Probably not past the Fourth of July," Scott said, putting his plate aside. "Guys, I need to run over some last-minute items in case something comes up at home. Lance, do you have any new information on the activities of that ex-gay group?"

"The director of that program asked that we provide a place for them to stand with their banner that says something like 'Jesus Loves You.' I helped them get that approved through the board."

"Good for you. What will a sign hurt?" Scott then looked at his photographer. "Make sure you get plenty of shots that will appeal to the locals. Later we can use them to sell ourselves when some fundamentalist tries to talk about how perverted we are. Okay?"

He was about to say something when his pager went off. Scott looked at the number.

"It's Annie. On your way out please tell Chris to hold all my calls until I finish with whatever is going on at home."

FIRST CHURCH, AUSTIN

Sitting alone in his office, Samuel Phillips took a strip of paper out of his wallet. He kept Scott's phone numbers hidden between two photos of Natalie. A churning raged in his gut.

What if Scott won't talk with me?

Samuel wanted to reject memories of the last time he saw his only child and the horrible words he had said to him. He knew God was not pleased.

Esther had begged Samuel to call his son during the last week of Natalie's life. She reminded him that he had talked to presidents and governors, so what was so hard about calling Scott?

"4-0-4," Samuel whispered softly. His hand shook while punching in the numbers. The phone rang four times before a cheery voice answered.

"May I help you?" the voice asked. She asked a second time.

"May I speak with Scott Phillips, please?" His chin quivered.

"Mr. Phillips is on another line, but if you'll hold, I'll put you through when he's finished."

An advertisement for the newspaper played as Samuel waited for Scott. In the recesses of his mind for the last few weeks God had showed him a door. Two minutes later the line was picked up again.

"I'm sorry, but Mr. Phillips is still on a call. May I take your name and number and have him call you back within the hour?"

Samuel sat frozen.

"Sir, are you there?" The voice was still pleasant but inquisitive.

"I'll call back later."

Samuel put down the phone before he had a chance to thank her. God wouldn't leave him alone. He had been running all these years from the door. If he was to have peace he must open it and let God have his time with him.

10

HALLTON — LATE MORNING

WAYNE PAID LITTLE ATTENTION to his work as he thought about Alex. Annie spoke highly of Scott and was encouraged by Alex's progress in the time she had been there. Today, however, he sensed more needed to be done.

"What should we be doing, Father?" Wayne hoped he was praying loud enough to be heard in his deserted field.

It wasn't long before he got his answer.

"Dad, are you okay?" Brian asked when his father came into the yard. While cutting the lawn Brian had been watching him walk from the field. Wayne picked up a garden hose and rinsed off his hands as he spoke.

"We need to talk. Call your brother, and I'll meet you on the front porch."

The family was soon assembled. The boys wondered what caused their father to stop work, especially since this was the first day in a week without rain.

"We need to talk about Alex," Wayne said. "I guess first thing I need to address: Alex is gay. We've avoided it, denied it, and tried to forget it. We must accept it as reality."

They nodded.

"Secondly, it's our fault Alex hasn't come home. I take responsibility for not reconciling with him at your grandfather's funeral. Mom and I hurt him, and it caused deep anger. I also need to do something to repair the damage. I feel it should be more than a simple apology," Wayne said as he thought. His eyes scanned the horizon before looking at his sons again.

"Before I say anything to Mom, what do you think about inviting Alex home?" Wayne asked, and then added, "That would also include Scott."

"People are already going to be talking about Mom going down there," Brian said, "so I guess I really don't mind."

"Yeah, because you'll be going to college next year; I still have to live here," Ben chided as he threw an empty gum wrapper at him.

"Ben's right, our decision could harm your friendships. That's why we need to talk about potential problems."

"I've never seen guys kiss—and *don't* want to," Ben said.

"I never have either, son, but I'm hoping we can treat them with respect, regardless," Wayne said.

Ben put his finger down his throat and pretended to gag. Brian took Ben's head in his hand and quietly said, "Listen to Dad, this isn't a joke." Ben then mouthed, "I'm not joking!"

"Pay attention," Wayne rebuked Ben. "When Alex dies, we'll need to support Scott—there'll be no laughing behind his back for *any* reason. Most of our friends won't agree with any of this."

"Uncle Jett won't agree," Ben said quickly. The Whitley boys felt a kinship with Jett because of the relationship he had had with their grandfather. However, The Coach pushed the boys to refer to Jett as a member of the family.

"Yeah, he said gay people deserve to die of AIDS," Brian added. "But I don't believe Uncle Alex deserves to die."

"Neither do I," Wayne said. "We don't need to know why Alex is where he is; we just need to do what the Lord tells us."

"Uncle Alex has sent us some really cool stuff for our birthdays; he must be a good guy," Ben said.

"The kid is right, Dad," Brian said as he patted Ben on the head. "When I do something wrong and then promise you I'll do better—the first thing you say is 'show me.' Let's show Uncle Alex we care."

"I'll be embarrassed, but I guess I'll live through it," Ben said with dread in his voice.

"Are you sure, Ben?" Wayne asked seriously.

"Yeah."

Wayne thought about the situation for a minute, and then he spoke. "I'll call Mom and tell her we're in."

"How do we explain this to people?" Brian asked. "Sooner or later my friends will be asking."

"From here on out we're going with God, and we don't need anyone's approval. Okay?"

Brian and Ben nodded.

"Then let's pray." Wayne bowed his head. It was past lunch before they finished their prayer.

ATLANTA ∼ THURSDAY EVENING

Back in the kitchen, Annie buried her face in her hands as she prayed. "God, please let me go home. I'm not able to handle this anymore."

Annie was unable to conceal her disgust any longer. Until today, everything had been going smoothly enough. She was grateful to Scott for providing information so conversations with her brother came easy. Last night Scott took her to see Alex's law firm while his friend Kerry stayed with Alex. If only The Coach had been able to put aside his prejudices for a moment to see how much Alex had accomplished, surely he would have been proud; Annie was.

The day began with Annie waking from a bad dream. Going outside to drink her morning coffee, she accidentally grabbed a copy of Scott's newspaper. *The Pride Position* was worse trash than any magazine she had seen at the grocery store checkout stand. The articles were disturbing and partisan. Fundamentalist Christians were portrayed as off-base radicals, the root of all society's ills.

What sort of mind would write those things? Have I misjudged Scott? He must accept this garbage because he's the owner and editor.

Annie pulled her hair as she watched the clock, waiting for Wayne's evening call. The phone rang, and she shouted an angry, "Hello!"

"Is something wrong?" It was Wayne.

"I want to come home." She began to cry as she sat down at the table. Annie hoped Wayne would tell her to board the next plane.

"What's happened? Is Alex well enough for you to leave?"

"I can arrange for a volunteer to take my place. I can't take this gay business anymore. All we wanted was for me to try, and I've failed."

"Tell me about your day," Wayne prompted. He would have to put off telling her about his talk with the boys.

"This afternoon Alex had some visitors, two men who were obviously together—you know what I mean. The younger one was a teenager, and the older man was in his late fifties. It was disgusting.

"Right this minute there's a couple—listen to me! Wayne, I sound like one of them. I'm talking like I approve of this thing between people of the same sex. Well, I don't! Do you hear me?" She was almost screaming by the time she finished her last sentence.

"What's going on?" Wayne had never heard Annie so distraught.

"One man is in black leather. The other one—Re'kae—has a wedge cut and his hair is bleached yellow. He's wearing—I don't want to talk about it. I thought Re'kae was a girl when I first saw him. I can't stay here no matter how much I love Alex."

"Sweetheart, please don't run. You could be at the point of God working in the lives of Alex and Scott."

"Don't give me that syrupy garbage. I've failed and I'm coming home."

"Okay, okay. The boys and I will pray. If God wants you to stay, then you'll know beyond a shadow of a doubt by tomorrow."

Maybe this was what Wayne was concerned about earlier in the day. He could have been sensing that Annie needed to come home.

"I just heard Scott drive in. He's early. I've got to leave for a while to think this through. Please pray, Wayne, I need it more than ever."

Annie hung up the phone. She dried her tears and then gathered her purse and the keys to Alex's car. Scott greeted her on the porch with a weary smile. His tie was loose and his suit crumpled. He had been at work for fourteen hours.

"Lesley sent me home. She's finishing up at the office. Where are you off to?"

"I've got to clear my head." Annie's voice sounded angry. "Dinner is in the oven."

"What's wrong? I saw the car out front. Who's here?" Scott grabbed her arm, but Annie jerked it away.

"Stuart and Re'kae! Good-bye!" she shouted from the driveway.

As Annie burned out of the driveway, Scott's heart sank. He went inside armed for battle, and by the time he got to the den he was steaming.

"Well, look what the cat dragged in," Stuart said.

Alex sat on the sofa enjoying the company. Scott eyed the guests with disgust. Stuart returned the stare with a haughty look, mumbling "pathetic" under his breath.

"Guess it's time to go." Stuart walked past Scott to shake Alex's hand. "You're looking good, old buddy. Keep thinking positive and you'll beat it."

"You never change, Scott," Stuart growled as he grabbed Re'kae's hand. "Don't bother showing us out."

After the door closed Scott spun toward Alex.

"What the hell is the matter with you? Haven't I told you not to let those degenerates come here? I can't believe you would do it now with Annie in the house."

"Jealous? Just pack your bags and get out of my house." Alex tied his blue plaid cotton robe around his waist and reached for his walker.

"*Our* house and those two guys are not welcome here. Understand? They're drug pushers, and that's the nicest thing I can say about them." Scott walked in front of Alex as he was trying to get up from the couch.

"Pardon me, Mr. Freedom of Speech Editor, but they're my clients. This happened to be a pleasant visit. When I get better I can go back and continue their case."

Alex stood up and pushed at Scott. He moved to let Alex feel he had won. Allowing Alex his turtle-paced mobility gave Scott time to cool off and think.

"And their guilt hasn't been proven," Alex said.

Scott burst into a rage.

"Get off of it, Marshall. We've both seen the tape of Stuart selling drugs to high school kids, so quit being sanctimonious. They're into the kind of stuff that kills people. Why are you so taken with those slime balls?"

"Talk about being sanctimonious. I think I've been wrong about you all along. Annie was nice to them. She's been nice to all my friends."

"What other friends? Who else has been here?" Scott panicked.

"Mandy and Tim." Alex gave Scott a condescending look.

"Mandy the child molester? My God! I don't want them in this house either. You shouldn't have represented that man. You know what he is. Maybe Tim had a horrible situation at home, but you allowed that child to go from the frying pan into the fire." Scott followed Alex down the hall to the kitchen. "Your heart is big, Alex, but just because they're gay doesn't mean what they do is right. Sometimes your generosity isn't wise."

As an attorney Alex had all sorts of clients. Scott had long ago told Alex that their home was off limits to many of these people.

"I don't need you anymore now that I have Annie. You can just leave." Alex opened the door and wobbled out to the deck, shutting it behind him.

Scott didn't know what to say. He walked to the window and observed Alex laboring to sit down. The dog was nosing Alex's hand as it reached for the chair. His beloved Alex's time was so short that any problem must be resolved quickly. As he was ready to go out and settle the argument, Scott stopped to answer the phone. It was Kerry.

"I was by the house today, and do you know who was there?"

"Yeah, I just found out. Why does he insist on being friends with those men?" Scott repeatedly ran his fingers through his hair.

"They boost his ego. He knows his career is over, so Alex grabs for anything that makes him feel significant. Anyway, I wanted to tell you that Annie's eyes were blazing. Mandy and Tim were pretty disgusting. I hinted for them to stop, but it didn't work."

"Eyes blazing, huh? I don't know what I'm going to do."

"Has she said anything?" Kerry asked.

"She went out for a breather, and she's real upset," Scott confided, and then added, "I've got to figure out some way to get her to stay."

Scott hunted around the kitchen for the food he smelled. Finding it in the oven, he held the phone with his chin while he took the casserole out.

"Whoa. Is this a new Scott talking?"

"I'm desperate." He grabbed a soft drink from the refrigerator. "Now, if you'll excuse me I have to figure out a plan."

Scott walked over to the window to see how Alex was faring.

"All right, buddy," Kerry replied. "If you need anything tonight I can be there in five minutes."

Scott was pensive as he walked onto the deck.

"I love you, but don't criticize my friends," Alex said as Scott sat down beside him.

"I'm concerned that Annie might not see our life as we see it. She needs to be—protected from extremes. Putting our best foot forward will help our cause. Annie's very conservative." Scott took Alex's hand. "Once she leaves . . ."

"She isn't leaving," Alex said.

Scott drew Alex's hand closer. "She'll be going back to her husband and children, and then I'll throw you a huge party. Right now let's enjoy her while she's still here—and be a family. Please?"

"Where's Annie now?"

"Out—she needed some air." Scott tried to sound happy. "She left dinner for us. We need to spend time by ourselves. Okay?"

Alex nodded and rubbed the dog's back.

Scott smiled and stood up. "Stay seated and I'll be back in ten minutes."

He walked back into the house. Alex had calmed down and appeared agreeable to limiting company. The bigger issue was getting Annie to remain in Atlanta. Scott closed his eyes and prayed.

"God, please let Annie stay. I've got to have her here. Whatever it takes, God, I'm willing."

II

ATLANTA ~ A SHORT TIME LATER

ANNIE DROVE TWO BLOCKS before she pulled over. The disgust, anger, frustration, and hurt poured out in hot tears. She begged the Lord to allow her to go home. Jett was right about Alex. He had no desire to give up homosexuality. She had begun to let down her barriers. Another week in Atlanta and there was no telling what she would accept. Alex and Scott looked respectable but were as deviant as the men who visited Alex today.

"Father, let me go back to Hallton," Annie prayed. "I'll serve you anywhere else, but not in this place."

She threw her head back against the headrest of Alex's Mercedes. Annie's right hand touched her Bible. Wiping the tears from her eyes, Annie picked it up from the passenger seat.

"Give me a verse to sustain me through the night. I must have it or I think I'll die."

She thumbed through the Bible several times. She felt deserted. As her eyes closed Annie saw herself in the room with Wayne, Clark, and Jett. Clark was saying that Alex needed to see Jesus.

How can I be unconditionally loving toward Alex, yet remain biblical without compromise? God, please show me, Annie asked God, but she really didn't want to know the answer. She just wanted to leave this place.

The Morningside area where Alex and Scott lived was dotted with rainbow flags flying from doorposts. Annie had become an authority on those things after a week. Rainbow flags meant the home belonged to a gay couple or that its inhabitants were gay-friendly.

"Pride Week," she said with disgust. "Lord, I really want out of this town."

Determined not to go back to Alex's until she had an answer from God, Annie found a restaurant. She asked the hostess for a quiet booth close to the door and the phone. Once she knew what to do, Annie would call Wayne to let him know so they could make plans. Right now Annie hoped the plans would be to return home by the weekend.

TAYLOR HOME, HALLTON

"Jett returned to the field after a little heart-to-heart with The Bear. As we lined up for the final play of the game I started thinking about how much I hated playing football in the cold rain." Harley was in his famous story-telling mode. This one was about a time when he and Jett played football for the University of Alabama.

"As usual when he starts to think, it was a disaster," Jett laughed and winked at Kitty. Harley's tale managed to take Jett's mind off the Whitley situation.

Jett jumped into the story like a player on the field. "Just as I was about to call the play I heard Harley say, 'I think there's some sick need in our lives that we get coaches who have *the* before their name.'"

"Jett shouted 'What?' and it confused the Auburn boys so much that they jumped offside, and their coach went nuts on the sidelines," Harley said as he mimicked the Auburn coach waving his arms.

"Because of him I was in major trouble with The Bear," Jett added.

"*And* The Coach was upset, too. He showed up to surprise us. Nag, nag, nag all the way through dinner," Harley said. "If fun were food The Coach would have been anorexic. I almost quit football."

"Instead you got the MVP award at the bowl game a month later." Jett smiled at Harley, but the mention of The Coach suddenly put a damper on his mood.

Jett was the son of an unwed high school dropout who had moved back to Hallton just before he started first grade. Harley's father was president of the bank, and coupled with his mom's inheritance, they were the wealthiest family in town. Despite their differences, Jett and Harley had been inseparable from the first day of school.

They loved trading old football stories. Before dinner the men played a short game, and it was evident they still possessed the magic that had made them superstars at every level of football.

"Well, before we go inside, Harley and I have some news about our family." Kitty grabbed her husband's hand and then quickly said, "We're having a baby."

"That's so wonderful; congratulations," Donna said excitedly. Jett was silent.

"Thanks. We couldn't be happier, and actually the girls are, too," Kitty replied. She waited a bit for Jett to respond before saying, "Donna, are you ready to go inside and make the dessert?"

Donna nodded. Harley began talking as the women got out of their chairs to start clearing the table.

"We asked the twins about another baby before I came back home. They're teenagers, and life is hard enough when you're that age with a father who's had very public moral failings. Kitty and I didn't want to add any embarrassment to their lives."

Jett and Donna understood. Besides the local gossip, there was always something on television about Harley's illegal, unethical acts. His older daughters had a hard time forgiving. Reunification had been a painful, two-year process—Jett had worked with the twins to help them resolve issues with their father.

"Well, congratulations, tough guy." Jett sounded disinterested. He asked Donna if she needed help in getting the dishes to the kitchen.

"You fellows just talk; we can take care of everything. Could you get the children out of the pool, Jett?" Donna asked, following Kitty through the sliding glass doors. She turned and was able to almost shut the door with her elbow.

Jett's commanding voice sent the children scurrying, and then he sat down again. Harley would now be privy to what had kept Jett so preoccupied most of the evening. The news of the Hamilton baby should have brought more of a response from him—Jett loved children.

Once he was sure no one would hear, Jett spoke, and his voice was full of loathing. "Alex Marshall is dying of AIDS. Annie's gone down to Atlanta to help out."

"Oh no!" Harley was shaken by the news. "Jett, when did you find out?"

"Wayne and Annie came by the church on Memorial Day to tell Clark and me. I haven't told anyone except Donna. Such a waste," Jett said, with contempt.

"What do you mean by waste? Because of the damage you did to Alex?" Harley was irritated.

Donna came to the door to finish closing it and heard the agitated tone of the men's voices. Harley hadn't raised his voice like that to Jett in years.

"Damage I did? Don't give me that garbage. Alex was lucky to have The Coach as his father and he blew it. He turned his back on everything God gave him." Jett would not make eye contact as he spoke.

"Jett, I don't know what you said to Alex the night before he left, but it must have been bad. It's because of you he . . ."

"I told him the truth," Jett interrupted Harley. "No one had the courage to do it but me. Why can't you come to grips with the fact that Alex Marshall is an unrepentant homosexual? He has been like this since I can remember. All our years growing up he would cling to us and follow us around with a weird sort of stare."

"Did it ever occur to you that we were so thick we had no room for anyone else? I think it's admirable that Annie went to Atlanta. So just lay off. If he comes back with her, leave them alone." Harley turned to Jett and caught a glimpse of Donna standing at the door.

"Annie won't bring him back. The Whitleys aren't fools. Alex gave himself over to a reprobate mind years ago."

"The Whitleys trust you, Jett. Don't get involved. I'm sure Annie doesn't know *everything*, or do I need to be more specific? I think she'd be curious to know what drove her brother away that night in Green Bay." Harley was nose-to-nose with Jett.

"I'll challenge anyone if it goes against the will of God, and that includes you." Jett was irritated.

This clearly wasn't the man who had worked so hard to save his own family. Additionally, Jett had given Harley some form of encouragement every day as he transitioned back into the community. Harley was at a loss.

"You stood by me when everyone thought I wasn't worth saving. Let the Whitleys hear God without you calling on the name of the late, great Bill Marshall," Harley said gently. "You know better than anyone that Annie and Wayne follow God."

Harley got up to warn Donna he was finished with the conversation. "I'm going inside to play with the kids. Please, give the Whitleys their chance with Alex, Jett. That's all I'm asking of you."

Donna walked toward the pantry. Inside the dark little room she caught her breath. She wondered if God had placed her at the door that moment to give her insight into her husband's rigidity.

What did Harley mean, "that night in Green Bay"?

PHILLIPS HOME, AUSTIN

It had been a long day for Samuel Phillips. Esther took phone messages while Samuel focused on writing letters—letters the Lord prompted him to send to people he had wrongly advised or hurt. One was a letter of apology to the working mothers in the church regarding the unnecessary guilt he had placed on them. He also wrote Brent a letter to reconfirm his offer of help. Before Samuel left the office he called Candace to encourage her to stay strong during this difficult period of separation from her husband.

The sun was setting on Austin as Samuel pulled into the driveway of his comfortable brick home near the University of Texas campus. On the radio Harry Chapin's song "The Cat's in the Cradle" played. The song was about a father who had no time for his young son, and then when he was old the roles switched. It reminded Samuel of his own life.

The garage door opened, and Samuel drove in beside the car Natalie used to drive. The car always roused his nostalgia. He married the blonde teenager the week after their high school graduation. It had been love at first sight when they met at a church camp. God had just called him to be a preacher, and together they prayed he would bless Samuel's ministry.

Samuel went through college and seminary on student loans and part-time jobs. Natalie's pregnancy with Scott was a surprise. Born the last year of college, he was to be their only child. A daughter was stillborn, and other pregnancies ended in miscarriages. Guilt engulfed Samuel as he realized how little attention he had given Natalie throughout those years.

Immediately after seminary Samuel took on the challenge of rebuilding the membership of an older church in Austin. Before their eyes Natalie and Samuel saw the answer to their prayers. Not in their wildest dreams had they thought God would bless them with the kind of growth their church experienced. From a core membership of less than two dozen, they built the church to the present-day membership with state of the art facilities. Natalie had been at his side the whole way, and now he was lost without her.

Tonight Samuel had gone home without stopping at her grave. Once he put his things down on the sofa, he walked up the stairs to the second-floor landing. He had not been in his son's room since the discovery of Scott with Chad Masters. Samuel had convinced Natalie to move their bedroom to the ground floor—he didn't want to walk past Scott's room each day and be reminded of what had happened to his family.

Why did I come home that day? Why did I defend Chad Masters?

The questions cut through Samuel's heart. Even when he had to fire Chad, it didn't compel Samuel to ask Scott's forgiveness. It took almost fifteen years for Samuel to admit he was wrong for what he had done: wrong for not hearing Scott's side of the story; wrong for not allowing Natalie an opportunity to help turn that moment of discovery into a pulling together of their family.

Samuel swung open the door to Scott's room. When he turned on the light, seeing the room took him back fifteen years to that moment of confrontation. All this time Samuel had assumed he would see it again through his own eyes, but God chose for him to relive the scene through the eyes of Scott. What a terrible father he had been.

Oh, my God, Samuel cried from deep within his soul.

He sat down on the plaid bedspread and looked at every square inch of the room.

"What have you done to me?" Samuel had shouted as he slapped Scott repeatedly. *"You're an abomination to God!"*

Scott's earthly image of God was Samuel, and he had beaten him without mercy—not only with his fists but with his words. Using God's name had been the knockout blow to crush his son's spirit. If he were honest, it had started before that afternoon—Samuel was a harsh and critical father.

On the shelf sat Scott's worn basketball. As Samuel's hands went around it, waves of sorrow swept him into another ocean of guilt. So many times his son had asked him to play, but he was always too busy.

God called parents to raise their children. Samuel's own words chastised his soul. Over the years he had preached dozens of sermons on the duty of parents to their children, and he had never heeded his own advice.

Still holding the basketball, Samuel's eyes caught the reflection of a small metal cross on Scott's bookshelf. He recognized it as something Scott made one summer in Vacation Bible School. When Scott rushed to show him, Samuel didn't even take it in his hands or give it a second look. Instead he kept talking to a person that now he couldn't remember their name or problem. Samuel had always focused on what made him look good, and now he realized his self-righteous pride had been a stench in God's nostrils. Why did it take losing his wife and son for him to wake up?

Samuel closed his eyes. "Please, Jesus, take care of my son," Samuel uttered in a whisper.

12

THREE SQUARES AND A SNACK, ATLANTA

Settling into the booth, Annie ordered hot tea and pulled her Bible from her purse. She read a few chapters of Psalms before she began the New Testament. God would direct her path. Annie hoped the direction would be home to Wisconsin.

Minutes became a couple of hours when Annie noticed a young couple enter the restaurant. With them was an older man dressed in layers of threadbare clothing and reeking of the street. As he shuffled off to the restroom to wash his hands and face, the couple took the booth next to Annie's. The evening manager approached their table and asked the couple to leave with their friend. The male diner explained how much money he and his business friends spent each week in this small eatery. He reasoned that with less than a dozen customers eating at this late hour, their guest should be welcome. Finally the manager gave in.

What courage it took to bring someone so dirty into a place where people eat, Annie thought.

The couple was oblivious to people's stares. The waitress asked if Annie would like to move, but Annie refused, knowing this was what God wanted her to see. Tonight was God's gift for the homeless man.

After the man told the couple his name was Edward, he explained that years ago he lost his job, and then soon after his wife became ill. In a short time their savings were drained, and her funeral put him into a financial hole. He had no relatives to fall back on and had been too proud to work at a minimum wage job. His last bit of money was invested in a get-rich-quick scheme, and before long he was on the street and penniless. Edward's cap to the story pierced Annie's heart: "I'm a worthless piece of trash."

The woman replied, "No one is worthless. You're a child of God and made in his image. God has a purpose for your life."

Annie didn't hear anymore. When she glanced down at her Bible, Matthew 25 lay open before her. The words were the same ones Sharon Robbins said to her the night Alex came home:

For I was hungry and you gave me something to eat, I was thirsty and you gave me something to drink, I was a stranger and you invited me in, I needed clothes and you clothed me, I was sick and you looked after me, I was in prison and you came to visit me.... I tell you the truth, whatever you did for the least of these brothers of mine, you did for me.

The despair lifted instantly. Annie saw her purpose for being in Atlanta. Alex and Scott were made in the image of God, and they had worth to him without changing anything in their lives. Yes, Annie could love them unconditionally.

"Lord, I've treated them as though they didn't deserve your love. Forgive me, Father," Annie prayed as she rushed for the pay phone. As soon as Wayne answered she said, "I'm staying."

"What happened?" Wayne asked.

"God changed my heart. I've wanted Alex to change so I can love him again. But I just need to love Alex and let Jesus handle the rest."

"The Lord has been showing me the same thing, Annie," Wayne said. "Only Jesus has the power to change a person's heart."

Annie nodded in agreement as if Wayne were there beside her.

"Wayne, all the years we've shut Alex out, he probably felt that God closed the door on him, too."

"Annie, what do you think about bringing Alex home? I mean here to Hallton—he needs a chance to make peace with his past," Wayne said.

"Are you serious?" Annie was caught off-guard. "What about the boys? Are they okay with this?"

"We want him to be with us until the end. The boys should have a chance to know their uncle. We also want Scott to come."

"Are you sure? What about their relationship?" Annie was excited but cautious.

"What kind of relationship do we have with Christ if we can only be around other Christians? I've got the rooming details worked out: Alex can stay in The Coach's old room and Scott can sleep in the room next door. Annie, it's time we start living a transparent life. We talk about it all the time in church—showing unconditional love, and now it's time to start doing it," Wayne finished.

"Oh, yes, I say yes—it's late, and I must get home to apologize to Scott because I was so nasty when I left. Give the kids my love. I love you, Wayne. I'll call when I've spoken with Scott and Alex."

Annie hung up the phone, paid the tab, and ran out of the restaurant.

13

MARSHALL-PHILLIPS HOME, ATLANTA

"ALEX, I WON'T LET YOU DOWN," Scott whispered to himself. For two hours he had wrestled with the gut-wrenching fear that Annie would return with plans to leave Atlanta.

Scott sat under an ancient oak tree in the front yard armed with a phone and room monitor; he would wait one more hour before finding someone to sit with Alex so he could look for Annie. Alex had no idea of Annie's emotional condition when she left the house, and for now that was best.

Two weeks ago Scott would have welcomed any opportunity to get rid of Annie, but he had become attached to her. It was hard enough to admit his willingness to compromise to keep her in town. But the bigger pill was that Scott knew he needed Annie's strength to carry him through Alex's death.

Shortly after eleven o'clock Annie pulled into the driveway and waved. Scott rushed to the car and flung open her door.

"I was so worried about you." He embraced her.

"I had to search for some answers," she said as they moved toward the house. "Scott, forgive me for being rude when you came home from work."

They walked through the foyer into the dimly lit kitchen. Scott turned on the light over the range as Annie sat down at the modern steel kitchen table. Seeing her remarkable calm, Scott feared she had resolved to leave.

"I know you've been awake since before dawn, but we need to talk," Annie began once he was seated in front of her.

"Could I say something first?" Scott interrupted. "You didn't need to be exposed to what you saw today. I'm sorry for what happened, and I promise it won't happen again."

Annie started to speak, but Scott held up his hand.

"Alex has a big heart. All those men are—were his clients. I've known Stuart since I came to Atlanta, and we intensely dislike each other. Stuart sells drugs and whatever else to make a living. That's how Alex came to represent him."

Scott kept talking as he got up to get a cola. "Re'kae dresses that way to make himself more attractive to Stuart. I came from a normal Christian home like Alex, so I can't relate to these men. I'm still struggling to be more accepting myself."

Scott nervously cleared his throat.

"Earlier today you met Mandy and Tim. Mandy—or Armand—is your stereotypical Southern gentleman who was a closet queen. In his younger years he taught high school English in a small Georgia town until the school board found out about his sexual preference. His family had neither the money nor the political ties to keep him from getting fired. A funny thing about the South: if you're rich, people overlook such things," Scott laughed. "Mandy lacks a certain refinement that most old Southern gentlemen possess when they're gay."

"I'll say," Annie chimed in.

"Honestly, Annie, I shouldn't laugh. It's a difficult life for a man like Mandy—he's raised by a mother who dreams he'll possess the refined gentleman qualities of Ashley Wilkes from *Gone with the Wind*. This same son will be rejected when he becomes a marvelously talented Cole Porter–type who obviously won't make her a grandmother."

Annie understood.

"Tim was twelve when he met Mandy. Tim's parents were either prostituting or hopped up on drugs—I can't remember. Because of Tim's unruly conduct and being an older adolescent, he was hard to place in foster care.

With Alex's help, Mandy won custody. I remember seeing Tim just after Alex took the case. He had open sores from cigarette burns by his parents and was malnourished. If all that wasn't enough, his uncles had routinely molested him for years."

"Twelve is Ben's age," Annie said softly. She couldn't imagine anything like that happening to either of her sons.

"And now he's Brian's age—it's Brian, isn't it—your oldest son?" Scott said. "I feel sorry for Tim, but I can't endorse a minor being in that kind of a relationship with an older man no matter what the circumstances."

Scott's voice became compassionate. "Kerry told me about their visit, and I'm so sorry. Alex knows they aren't welcome here. I've told him that he needs to be careful, but he only wants to help ease the pain he sees in people."

Annie was touched. "Is this typical in the homosexual community?"

"What?" Scott had no idea what she meant.

"Is it typical for homosexuals to experience extreme things happening to them?"

"The right-wing community believes all of us have experienced an over-bearing mother, a bad father-son relationship, or were molested. The one thing that's true is many of us have received abuse at the hands of those who are closest to us in the heterosexual world. Straight people—mainly conservative Christians—who think we're less than human."

"I know we hurt Alex. Did the same thing happen to you?"

"I don't talk about it. In my business I keep my personal life to myself. People get the information and then use it to hurt you. I consider my life before Alex nonexistent."

"Forgive me."

"For what? Annie, you've brought life back to Alex." Scott drew a breath, because sharing his feelings was difficult. "I was opposed to you coming."

Annie smiled. "You weren't the only one. I fought it all the way."

"I was worried that you might come between Alex and me." Scott was finding it easier to open up. "Once you got here you were so much like Alex that I felt I'd known you for years. You didn't judge us, even though you were uncomfortable."

"I've never been around gay people. I'd never have been able to handle Alex's illness without you."

The rosewood clock down the hall struck midnight. Scott looked at Annie's face.

"Please stay."

"I'd like to, but . . ." Annie began.

"But you need to get home. I understand." Scott was overwhelmed with disappointment. "Your family needs you. Well, it's been . . ."

Annie offered a reassuring smile. "I grew up thinking there was a set of rules for everything. Compromise in my world is considered dangerous. Walking out of a Christian 'comfort zone' can be construed by others as compromise. God wants us to take risks, because Jesus never played it safe."

Scott was pleasantly amused and figured he would get a nicely milled Christian speech. "Let me fix a sandwich—I'm starving."

Annie nodded and then continued as Scott worked around the kitchen.

"Since Alex left I believed if I gave you all any attention, I'd compromise my beliefs. Not knowing you, I saw the two of you only through the context of your physical relationship. Earlier you mentioned you grew up in a Christian home. Are you a church-going person?"

Scott piled lettuce and tomatoes on his sandwich.

"I've darkened a few doors. From the fundamentalist perspective I've never asked Jesus into my life, because I saw too much hypocrisy from the pulpit. God has blessed me in my business, my life with Alex, and with good friends. What more could I ask?"

Scott had the urge to tell Annie who his father was. No one knew, not even Alex. In the last few days Scott had realized how important family was; however, she continued before he had a chance to say anything.

"Then I will speak directly: If I'd stayed tucked inside the walls of my church, I wouldn't have met Alex's friends today or known their stories. This week my faith in Jesus Christ has grown. It doesn't require any faith to get dressed for church and sit in a pew. Some of my Christian friends were skeptical about my trip and called it compromise. But it turned out to be an opportunity from God to grow spiritually."

Scott held tightly onto his sandwich. No conservative Christian had ever spoken to him with such clear insight. Annie was the sister he had imagined having when he was a young boy. Annie's eyes became serious, but the tone of her voice was genuine.

"God is showing us—Wayne, the boys, and me—that our years of separation have robbed us of a rich relationship with Alex and with you. We also believe God wants us to make up for lost time. We'd like for Alex and you to come to Wisconsin."

He started to object, but Annie motioned for him to stop.

"Hear me out," Annie said. "Alex needs the chance to make peace with his past. Are you able to move your office temporarily to our house? We'd like for you to stay until he passes away."

"Annie, when you left tonight the last thing I expected was for you to ask us to come to Wisconsin. You're very kind, but you *must* reconsider. You have *no idea* what could happen if you take us into your home. Well-meaning people can create a lot of trouble for you. It would be social suicide for your family in your Christian community."

"Our family is willing to take that risk. Please call Wayne tomorrow and discuss your business needs. I'd like for the three of us to go as soon as Alex has medical clearance," Annie said.

"Annie, you beat all." Scott would reason with Wayne tomorrow.

Scott wiped his mouth with his napkin. Annie took the cue.

"I'm exhausted and you must be, too. I'll clean the dishes in the morning. Goodnight." She hugged him and was off to her room.

As Annie settled in to her ritual of journaling before bed, she heard Scott shooting hoops. Outside in the warm night air Scott shot the basketball as if he was in the NBA finals.

She can't be serious. Wisconsin would never work. Get it out of your head, Scott. It will never work.

HAMILTON HOME, HALLTON

"What were you and Jett raising your voices about tonight?"

Kitty took down her long red hair and began brushing through the thick curls. Harley was propped up in bed with his Bible. In the distance was the sound of the draining bathtub.

Harley had been in deep thought since leaving the Taylor home. He sighed before answering her question.

"Alex Marshall has AIDS, and Annie is in Atlanta taking care of him."

"How sad for all of them." Kitty crawled to the middle of the bed and sat cross-legged while she finished her hair. "That must have been why Donna was fine one minute and distracted the next."

"She heard us talking. She doesn't know I saw her at the door, so please don't tell."

"Alex's situation shouldn't have any effect on Donna; she doesn't even know him really. What else did Jett say?" Harley's explanation did not seem logical.

"I said some things about how Jett treated Alex, and . . ." Harley closed his Bible before continuing. "The night before Alex left for Atlanta he came to see Jett."

Her eyes grew wide. "What happened?"

"Alex came to our hotel the night before a game. He knew that The Coach was always on Jett's visitor's list. I figure Alex used his dad's name to get to our floor—both of them being William Alexander Marshall. From the minute Jett saw Alex he ripped him apart. I tried to stop it, but he told me it was between the two of them. I left and there's no telling what transpired after that." Harley had lots of regret.

"What could Alex have said to Jett to create such a response, sweetheart?" Kitty stopped brushing her hair and rubbed his arm to comfort him.

"Alex said he had something to share from the Lord, and Jett didn't want to hear it." Harley gathered Kitty in his arms. "Kitty, the Whitleys have no clue Alex visited Jett that night. What should I do?"

"We can't force Jett to admit to anything. If the truth is to come to light, it will only happen through prayer."

"That's what we need to do—but first . . ." Harley was hesitant. "We need to talk, because there's something that I think you need to know about me."

"What?" Old feelings of being betrayed began to rise up in her.

"I can't deal honestly with Jett unless I get my life right . . ." Harley took a deep breath and began telling her the secret of his past.

14

MARSHALL-PHILLIPS HOME, ATLANTA

"BRIAN! BRIAN, YOU'LL NEVER GUESS what's happened." Ben burst through his older brother's bedroom door like a firecracker exploding.

Brian grabbed his alarm clock and looked at the time. It wasn't even seven o'clock yet.

"Batting practice isn't for three more hours. Leave me alone." Brian rolled over, putting the pillow over his head.

Ben jumped on top of him to wrestle the pillow away. After a minute Brian gave up on sleeping any longer. Brian was slow to anger and gentle with everyone—even this young ball of energy who was five years younger.

"It better be good, hot rod." Brian rubbed his face and shook it to try to fully wake up and hear the news.

"Uncle Alex is coming home! Scott just called Dad and said they would come. That means we're going to have two—uh—two guys in our house. Dad says we can't joke about it, but, Brian, that's just gross." Ben dramatically threw himself down on the bed.

Brian sat and thought before he spoke. "Well, think about this—Mom and Dad are going to be extra nice to us. We're, like, the best kids ever for going along with this."

"Brian, I'll be called a sissy!" Ben protested.

"Not you, slugger." Brian took off Ben's ever-present baseball cap and hit him over the head with a loving tap. "Anyway, you've got me to take up for you. I'm bigger than your friends. Don't worry, kid, I'll make sure you aren't bullied."

Ben relaxed a bit and then quickly asked, "But what about you? Who'll take up for you?"

Brian turned on the radio that sat on his bedside table so his father wouldn't overhear him.

"Well, if I'm going to take care of you, then I guess I'll be able to handle what's thrown at me." Brian smiled to try to reassure Ben.

Ben thought. Then he spoke with doubt mixed in his words as well as his voice. "You really think people will leave you alone?"

"I didn't say they wouldn't bother me. I hope no one bothers either of us." Brian sighed. "I know a couple of guys who might—well, it's summer and maybe they'll just forget where I live. Anyway, I've got a girlfriend now, and that should help."

"Maybe we need to go down to Atlanta and just forget about Mom bringing them back up here." Ben lay on his back and repeatedly threw the baseball toward the high ceiling, catching it in his glove. One almost hit Brian in the head.

"Watch it," Brian said when he was dodging the ball. "No, we need to have Uncle Alex here. I know Dad's right."

He got up from the bed. "I'm gonna go shower, and then I'll pitch you a few balls after breakfast."

As Brian grabbed his clothes to take into the bathroom, he thought about what was coming. He dreaded the talk and taunting that was sure to surface once his uncle arrived. Brian got picked on a lot already because he was so studious and didn't care for football.

People always told Brian he resembled Uncle Alex. As curious as he was to see how true it was, he worried that people would think he was gay, too. While he knew those comparisons were really about positive personality attributes, there were those who might turn it into more.

He got into the shower. Brian knew he could tough out another year in Hallton. His girlfriend—Stephanie Hamilton—had endured a good many unkind words about her father. Brian thought about calling her to go with him to Ben's batting practice. They could talk for the two hours Ben was busy.

It was going to be tough making sure Ben didn't suffer needless bullying from his friends. As if he didn't have enough to worry about. It was going to be a long summer.

ATLANTA

When Annie called Wayne, he told her Scott had reluctantly agreed to come if Alex was willing. Scott had also gotten on the phone and warned Wayne of problems that might arise by having a gay couple in their home, especially one dying of AIDS. Wayne assured him he'd rather deal with angry neighbors than to displease God again.

Alex began to stir as Annie finished her coffee. Putting the mug in the sink, Annie walked down the hall to his room. Today the walls were brighter and the atmosphere warmer. She felt like dancing into his room.

"Good morning. How are you doing?"

"A little weak," Alex replied. "I need some oxygen."

Alex was propped on pillows. Annie hooked the hose onto his nose and around the back of his head. The worry lines seemed to have disappeared from her face.

"You're doing very well. You mastered the walker yesterday, and slept without oxygen last night, so that's great progress."

"Are you leaving?" Alex felt well enough to be frank.

"Heavens, no, I told Scott last night I'm in this for the duration." Only when Scott was with them would she discuss Wisconsin. It might overwhelm Alex if she rushed with her news first thing.

"Duration? Like until I die?"

"Until I'm no longer needed, Alex," she said with an assuring tone.

For the first time Annie kissed his cheek without thinking about what man may have kissed it. God had truly changed her heart. She brought a pan of water to the bedside to help him freshen up after night sweats.

"What gives? You don't seem like yourself today." Alex was suspicious.

"Jesus got my attention last night," Annie said as she continued the morning ritual. "Since you left Hallton, I've seen you through jaded eyes. I don't blame The Coach—I had a free will. Whatever time we have left I want to spend with you and Scott."

Annie finished Alex's sponge bath and then proceeded to collect dirty clothes. She allowed time for her statement to sink in.

"Are you sure, or is this some religious gimmick to get me to repent before I die?"

Grabbing a large navy pillow from the lounge chair, Annie propped her back on the ornately tooled footboard.

"I think Scott is a wonderful man. He's filled me in on the part of your life that I missed, but now I want to get to know you again." Annie rubbed Alex's feet through the cover.

"But Scott and I are gay, Annie, and that's synonymous with hell." He sounded more like his old vigorous self. "A homosexual is what I am. You've told me my union with Scott is a sin. Are you still a Bible-believing Christian, or are you accepting my lifestyle? You can't have it both ways."

"There's more to you than homosexuality."

"But you've never wanted to see anything else. So how are you justifying the sin issue?" Alex asked.

"To the people in Hallton your lifestyle seems to be a very obvious sin." Annie was direct.

"And what about you? Are you suddenly going to say it isn't obvious to you?"

"Everyone has sin whether it's obvious or not. Mine was being sanctimonious when you needed me." Annie shifted on the bed. "Last night God showed me that you've always known where I stood biblically, Alex. I never let you know how much I love you."

Annie wiped her tears before she continued.

"God has shown me what I've done to you all these years. I can't make up for what Hallton did to you, Alex. The sins of people there aren't so obvious . . ."

"Hallton doesn't matter anymore," Alex inserted, and then his voice trailed off.

"Why?"

"When the rubber met the road, I had to admit I was born gay. The part that hurt so badly was people's reactions. Did God create me to go to hell?" He paused. "Annie, you don't have to answer. All my life I knew I was different. I never put everything together until I moved to Atlanta."

Alex rarely dwelled on the specific incident that propelled him to leave Wisconsin. In recent years Alex chose to believe that it was fate that sent him to Atlanta.

"To be honest, sis, it wasn't just the difference inside that caused me to leave. Moving here made me feel safe, because I was away from the taunts and jeers of the people in town. Most of my life I worried about someone hurting me whenever I was out.

"Annie, I'm not like the athletes who hung around our house. You know, I never received any affirmation from a guy until I came to Atlanta." Alex wiped the tears on the navy and tan cotton striped sheet. "For years I tried to convince the people of Hallton I had something to offer. No one ever noticed."

Annie gave Alex a tissue to blow his nose as she wiped her own tears. Her heart broke as he described what his life had been like in Hallton. She had seen the rejection by his peers, but she never knew the emotional toll it took on him.

"Ever wonder why our father had us call him 'The Coach'?" Annie asked. "'Daddy' was just too intimate for him to handle. I guess it made him feel vulnerable. Wayne and I are sorry we didn't step in earlier. Maybe it would have made The Coach shape up."

"Do you know, once I came to Atlanta I actually excelled in sport—the very thing he was always telling me I couldn't do right. Those trophies are proof—all awards for tennis, racquetball, and softball." Alex pointed to a dozen statues in a glass case. "In as many ways as I failed in Hallton I've achieved here."

"Just because you didn't meet The Coach's expectations doesn't mean you were a failure. You speak for those who can't speak for themselves. You fit God's mold. We just waited too long to realize it."

"Annie, I'm gay. I'm in love with a man, and I help gay people. I'm not a Christian by your standards."

"Outwardly, you don't appear to line up with the Word of God. But I believe God looks at what is inside of us and judges that. Only you know where you stand with the Lord."

"The Bible also says we're to judge our brothers who are in error," Alex said. "What about that?"

"If I stood before the Lord, he'd tell me I did things to you that closed your heart to him. Jesus would tell me I wasn't willing to humble myself and ask your forgiveness. You couldn't hear him because of how I treated you. Please forgive me, Alex."

Scott walked into the room. He greeted Alex and then kissed Annie on her cheek. Dropping down into the tan, polished-cotton chair, Scott looked at both of them under heavy lids. Annie turned back to Alex.

"Wayne and I want you both to come back to Hallton as soon as the doctor says you can travel. The boys—especially Ben—need a chance to know you. You need the opportunity for people to rectify the wrongs they've done to you."

Alex shook his head.

"It won't work. Too much has happened," he said.

Scott said, "I tried to tell her last night. I thought I might talk some sense into Wayne, but every turn I made the door opened wider for us to go."

"You don't understand. I *can't* go back." His heart beat furiously at the thought.

"You always wanted me to see the countryside." Scott took his partner's hand. "I've arranged for Lesley to manage the business while we're away. Dr. Moss sees no reason why you can't travel by next week. His only concern was finding a doctor who'd treat you."

"Wayne told me Kitty Hamilton has offered to do it," Annie said.

"And Kerry will take care of things on the home front, so there's nothing left to do but to go," Scott added.

Annie moved to the head of the bed to be beside Alex.

"You won't be the butt of one of The Coach's jokes. We don't care what anyone says, because we're confident this is what God wants us to do. If you get there and want to come back to Atlanta, I'll come with you." Annie hugged Alex. "And I'll stay until the end."

Maybe God wanted him to go back to Hallton. Alex had never trusted God like he wanted to trust him now. In the pit of his stomach, Alex feared what Jett might do to him once he was back on his turf. The fear of being humiliated was hounding him when he heard Annie's voice.

"No one will hurt you—or Scott. No one will get to you unless they come through us. You deserve to come home, Alex. Please, give it a chance."

Peace came to Alex like a candle lit in a cave. As small as the flame, light overtakes, and peace seemed to flood his whole body.

He heard himself mutter, "Yes."

15

HALLTON ~ SUNDAY MORNING, JUNE 12

"... AND WHEN WE ARE TEMPTED to judge, we must remember what Jesus did for us. He extended to us mercy, before we knew to ask for it." Clark finished his sermon with a sweeping gesture of his massive hands.

Wayne would be speaking to the congregation soon. He prayed that members would be receptive to him. Clark had vowed his support no matter what the reaction. At the end of the prayer Clark walked back to the center of the pulpit area. He motioned for everyone to be seated. The morning sun came through the windows. The three hundred seats were filled with teenagers and adults.

"Before we close, Wayne Whitley would like to speak to you. Please open your hearts and see how you can help the Whitley family in the upcoming days." Clark motioned for Wayne to come to the front.

"Friends, most of you know that Annie has been gone for about ten days to care for her brother, Alex. He was raised in this church, and it was at this altar that he committed his life to the Lord. Many of you remember that Alex worked for Community Challenge for three years before going to Atlanta."

As Wayne scanned the room, he caught Jett's piercing eyes cutting each word that came from his mouth.

"Alex went to Atlanta and took up the gay lifestyle." A ripple went through the crowd. "Since 1981 we've had little to do with him. But now he has AIDS, and in the last few days our family has sensed God wanting us to do more. Had Alex been a murderer, we'd have never alienated him."

Wayne continued when he saw Harley give a little nod.

"Our church rallied around Harley, and look at what the Lord has done," Wayne said, as he returned the nod as a thank you.

"Annie and I have been seeking the Lord, and we've decided to invite Alex to come back to Hallton. His time is short and he deserves to be at home when he dies. We're open to the Lord and doing his will. Friends, we request your prayerful support."

There was one more thing Wayne had to say. When he finished, the die would be cast, and the Whitleys' true friends would be revealed. Wayne watched Brian, anticipating his next words. How many parents would force their children to sever ties with his sons? It hurt to think that Ben could possibly be rejected by his baseball team.

Wayne's message had to be tempered with wisdom. "We've also invited Alex's companion. We know nothing about him, but we believe that God wants us to minister to Scott as well."

From his left he heard the voice.

"I can tell you about him—in fact, both of them. They're two unrepentant sodomites—blasphemers of God. I'm shocked at you, Wayne," Jett said.

Jett rose to his feet to meet Wayne head-on.

"What are you saying to your sons by allowing this? That it's okay to be gay?"

Wayne responded, "We aren't ignoring the type of bond these men have, but Jesus did radical things to reach people right where they were. We don't want Alex to curse us with his last breath for taking Scott from him. Nor do we want Scott to rail against God because we took his companion. Our children have seen what happens when a family cannot love with the love of Jesus. We aren't asking anyone to help with Alex; we're only asking for prayer."

"You and I both know The Coach wouldn't permit Alex to be brought back to Hallton, especially with his friend. This will contaminate all the families that come in contact with you. Please reconsider this very noble idea of yours."

Jett gained the allegiance of many with his eloquent speech. This was a typical tactic of Jett to win people to his point of view. It caused Wayne's anger to swell. Jett sounded just like The Coach.

"Like Scott, Jett, you know what it means to have the person you had planned to spend the rest of your life with die prematurely."

"Don't ever compare Alex's gay friend to Rita!" Jett was incensed. Everyone knew that years ago Jett's fiancée had committed suicide after a long battle with depression.

"Jett, I'm not going to pretend to understand homosexuality. But these men aren't animals—Jesus died for them, too. We're hoping Alex and Scott will come to know who they are in God's eyes through our care."

"Alex left the Lord out of his own free will. Rationalize it any way you want, Wayne. These fine people know I'm right. Sin like Alex's destroys families and the lives of those around him. I won't compromise the word of the Lord for any reason."

The words were becoming more explosive with each statement when Susan Spencer stood. Her trustworthiness was her bond with the community.

"While there's life in Alex's body, he needs to see us respond to him through acts of selfless love. I understand it takes a lot of work to care for an AIDS patient. For those who wish to assist, I'll prepare a chart for taking food to the Whitley home."

Susan smiled at the congregation. A few heads began to nod.

"It's been too long since any of us have done anything for Alex. You might have someone in your family who has strayed from the Lord. Use this opportunity of ministering to Alex to ask God to have Christians cross the path of your loved one. I'll have a signup list for everyone on Wednesday night."

Jett dropped down in the pew, shaking his head as the congregation whispered. Susan had been effective at taking the bite out of his words. Nonetheless, Wayne wanted to cry with frustration. Bill Marshall had given everything to Jett, and the least Jett could do was keep quiet about his feelings toward Bill's son. The whispers stopped as Clark stood.

"Let's pray for God to lead the Whitley family. Thank you, Susan, for your assistance." He waited a couple of seconds. "Dear Lord, as we depart today, we ask your protection and your blessings on each one here. In the name above all names, amen."

The congregation was dismissed.

FIRST CHURCH, AUSTIN

The piano and organ blared out the last stanza of "Just As I Am."

Rumors that Samuel had encouraged a woman to leave her husband for non-biblical reasons had flooded the community. Brent fueled the hearsay within the church by suggesting that Samuel had illicit intentions toward Candace. It seemed that all of Austin was interested in what Samuel Phillips had to say.

Finally it was time for the sermon. Samuel appeared calm and resolved as he ascended to the podium to speak. The church pianist got up and walked to Samuel's side. He was one of the very few church staff who supported Samuel.

"Over half my life has been given to this church—not just regular business hours, but evenings, nights, weekends, vacations." He had no smile. "In the last few weeks God has made me aware of my misplaced priorities.

"I made unnecessary sacrifices to build this church. Not just in time, but in trying to maintain my position within the community. For one, I never became involved in controversial issues when it was time to move into action. Just as a general should be at the front of his troops, a pastor must lead in every area—and not just with eloquent words from the pulpit. Please forgive me for not being there with you.

"Abuse is one area in which I've been silent. Through the years I've asked abused women to remain as a silent witness in the home—thinking that would cause their husbands to change. If I had taken time to look at the facts that were staring me in the face, I'd have known that the abuse never stopped.

"My advice was one-sided. In Ephesians, God told you men to lay down your life, your desires—everything for your wife. It isn't a suggestion but a command." Samuel took a breath, because his next words were painful. "Sometimes there are bruises no one sees, but they are felt just like a punch in the stomach—I was that kind of husband to my wife."

There were gasps and hushed whispers from the congregation.

"I think it's common knowledge that I maintained a strict household. I had Natalie attend to the needs of everyone else, but I neglected hers and our son's. Now, to my dismay, I see this replicated in our church. *I was wrong.*" Samuel pointed his finger and spoke with conviction.

"Our son . . ." Samuel had to regain composure before he could continue. "Scott was a beautiful, intelligent, and loving child. Brothers and sisters, I sinned as a father because I was never home. I never had time to notice what was happening in his life.

"Scott's departure was the result of my misplaced priorities as a father and as his pastor. He hated my Christianity so much he wouldn't consider asking Jesus into his heart."

Eubanks stood. "Samuel, you need to stop this."

"Gerald, you need to sit down." Samuel continued without taking a breath. Embarrassed, Eubanks sat down.

"Why would Scott want to be like me? He never received my attention, so he had to find it elsewhere. I sacrificed my real call—that of a parent and husband. I urge each man here to consider his ways. Submit your life to the examination of the Holy Spirit. With that said, I resign as your pastor effective immediately."

Samuel turned and walked from the podium to his office ahead of the press of the crowd.

16

JETT'S OFFICE

"What do you mean by bringing Alex and his friend to this town, Wayne?" Jett yelled.

"I had hoped you'd stand by me in this. Instead, you turned people against us. What's the matter with you?" Wayne asked.

Wayne had followed Jett into his office immediately after the service and closed the door. Jett stood behind his oak desk, cool and collected.

"I was only doing what any concerned Christian would do. You've gone off the deep end. I highly question your wisdom."

The Coach's number one protégé wasn't going to rattle Wayne.

"I really don't care what you think. We've only got a short time to show him the love of Christ, which for some reason he never saw in any of us."

"Alex chose not to see the love of Christ. He wouldn't submit to God's Word. God would have delivered him from sin if he'd only asked. Instead, he took his usual wimpy way out and let sin overtake him. This disease is the result of his years of rebellion. God gave it to him."

Wayne reached across the desk, grabbed Jett's collar, and tightened his fist around it. "Don't ever let me hear you say that again, not in a joke, not in a conversation, and not in a sermon. You owe that much to The Coach." Wayne loosened his grip on Jett.

"See what I mean? You've lost all reason. You've never gotten physical with me before." Jett readjusted his collar and pressed down his suit with his hands. "It's very nice of Annie to go see Alex, but bringing him home puts everyone at risk. Alex may be bedfast, but his friend can get around."

"Come off of it, Jett! Why are you assuming Scott is promiscuous just because he's gay?" Wayne looked at him and then added, "I could assume that since you were a pro athlete, you were sleeping around. Did you?"

Jett steadied his breathing so Wayne wouldn't see that a nerve had been hit. Sex with Rita wasn't sleeping around, but God kept subtly reminding him of his moral failure.

Surely what Wayne just said is a coincidence. God, why do you keep doing this? Don't you know I can't tell anyone? Jett battled God in his mind.

Wayne continued, not noticing any change in Jett's demeanor.

"Annie and I know we're doing what God wants us to. We're bringing Alex home to die, because it's the right thing to do. I'm not asking you to bring the youth group over to our house to watch a movie with Alex and Scott, but I do ask for your respect."

The door opened and Harley walked in but remained at a distance. Harley kept his eyes fixed on Jett. Jett returned Harley's icy gaze and then turned back to Wayne.

"I won't stay silent on this matter. The Coach wouldn't have consented, and I won't either. Wake up, Wayne."

"The Coach was a hardheaded old fool. We're in this predicament because that man couldn't love Alex unconditionally," Wayne said.

"Fine thing for you to criticize him now he's dead," Jett said. "Wayne, I have no complaint with you. I just don't want you to bring your brother-in-law back to this town. If you want to serve God, go serve him in Atlanta. Take the boys down there on a vacation, but don't bring that plague to our town."

"What's changed you, Jett? Three years ago you did a tremendous job getting people to believe in Harley again. Obviously, I didn't know you as well as I thought I did."

"Wayne," Jett said, "I stand by what I say. We don't need an upstanding deacon in our church entertaining unrepentant, disease-ridden, homosexual men in his home."

"Good day, Jett."

After Wayne left, Harley approached Jett.

"Leave them alone." Harley picked up the corner of the desk and shoved it into Jett's legs to vent his anger. Items on it rattled and papers fell on the floor.

"I'm glad Wayne and Annie have enough courage to bring him home," Harley continued. "You did something to Alex that night and only you know what it was. When Alex gets here I don't want to hear stories about how he fell from grace or see his head on your spiritual wall of persons who left God. Understand?"

"I did *nothing* to Alex," Jett said in a controlled voice.

"Something happened," Harley replied in a voice that was as controlled as Jett's.

"You were there, and I didn't say anything that we hadn't said before," Jett said defensively.

"We were insensitive to Alex and were part of his problem here in Hallton."

"Get real, Harley. Alex is still destroying lives with his sinful choices. He'll ruin Wayne, Annie, and their children before this charade is played out. Anyway, I don't want to hear your opinion on anything until you're honest with your wife—now put that in your pack of cigarettes and smoke it." Jett sneered.

"For your information, I told Kitty. But as excruciating as it's been for us to discuss it, I'm relieved she knows. I'm not hiding anymore," Harley said. "Jett, don't hide; go to Wayne and tell him about that night in Green Bay."

"Get out!" Jett's hand pointed to the door.

"Repent from what you've done and make it right. I will help you get through this in any way you need me to." Harley offered his hand to Jett, but it was refused.

Harley walked out. In the past he would have been arrogant, but today he spoke for Alex, Wayne, Annie, and God. Unknowingly he passed Donna in the hallway. She had overheard the whole conversation.

Harley has never challenged Jett before. If Jett hurt someone, he needs to make it right. She sat on a church bench a few feet from the office door that bore various Christian symbols. Jett was squeezing the life out of his relationship with the Lord and their family. He was so different from the man she married. Without thinking, Donna walked into the auditorium, where she found Wayne and Susan Spencer.

"Susan, let me bring food for their arrival. The Coach was so close to Jett that I want to be a part of helping you. When do you expect them, Wayne?"

"I expect them mid-week, probably Wednesday but at the very latest on Friday. It's very kind of you to offer your help."

Donna smiled.

"When we were missionaries, my parents and I ministered where there were many fatal illnesses. I don't share my husband's concerns about contagion. Susan, I'll call you this week. Wayne, I'm very proud of you and Annie. I promise to pray for you daily."

Donna left the auditorium. Neither Wayne nor Susan spoke. Even though she made it appear that her gesture was for The Coach, it was clear to them that Donna was obviously not submitting to Jett's wishes. She had never done anything like this before. Division was in the Taylor household.

17

HAMILTON HOME

"Did you tell Jett I'm going to be Alex's doctor?" Kitty began putting dishes into the dishwasher. Most Sundays their daughters would help clean up the kitchen, but today they were allowed to leave early so their parents could talk.

"I imagine he'll figure it out pretty soon." Harley scraped food from the plates.

"What do you think happened that night? I've never seen Jett as vicious as he was this morning in church. It's like overnight he's become The Coach."

"He was like this that night in Green Bay. I think Jett's afraid of Alex. Frankly, I'm glad Alex is coming back. I need to ask his forgiveness for a bunch of things I did to him over the years."

"Good. Someone needs to be the first to offer an apology," Kitty said.

Harley wiped down the round kitchen table. The old-fashioned kitchen with lots of windows, a fireplace, and a rocking chair was his favorite room in the house. The comfort of his huge country home made him content to stay on his farm. It had helped him forget the inhumanity of prison.

"I should have punched Jett's lights out that night. I'll never forgive myself for walking out and leaving Alex defenseless."

Kitty walked over to Harley and put her hand on his shoulder. He put down the damp rag. Sitting down in the rocker, Harley pulled her into his lap. Kitty spoke first.

"I need to go to Green Bay and talk with a colleague who works with AIDS patients. The girls have places they're going. Why don't you go see Aunt Susan? She's a wise woman. Tell her everything and see what she thinks."

"Good advice. Anything else?" he asked as he rocked her.

"Why don't you see what Wayne needs? He might need some help getting ready for Alex." Kitty smiled and then added, "As I listened to Jett this morning, I realized how much you've changed. Forgive me for being so angry with you the last few days. It took a lot of guts to tell me about that girl." Kitty played with Harley's golden hair.

"Thanks for your forgiveness—it's not easy to confess when you know it hurts the people you love," Harley said while giving her a big hug.

"Call Aunt Susan while I gather the girls, okay?" She kissed him and then called to the girls to get ready.

"I'm on it now." Harley turned to the desk by the rocker and picked up the phone.

TAYLOR HOME

"You've been very quiet. Is something wrong?" Jett asked Donna as they walked into the house after lunch.

The paintings on the refrigerator and the teddy bears on the sofa were reminders to Donna of how innocent life had been a few hours ago. Walking a few feet behind their son, Will, Donna did not respond to anything Jett was asking.

"Time for a nap, Will," Donna said. "I'll be in to check on you in a minute."

She continued down the hall to their bedroom as Will went into his. Harley's words were eating away at everything she held sacred about her marriage; topping the list was her expectation that Jett was an honorable man.

Jett followed her into the bedroom. Irritated by her lack of response to his questions, he had an edge to his voice. "Are you going to tell me what's wrong?"

"I overheard you with Harley when they were at our place for dinner." Donna was direct. "And I was outside your office this morning when he was begging you to come clean about Alex. I want to know what happened in Green Bay and why you haven't told Annie and Wayne."

"You were eavesdropping?" Jett asked.

"The door was open, both times, and you were loud." Donna sat at the foot of the bed. "Jett, I'm going to ask you a question, and I want you to be honest. When you were young *were* you and Alex ever . . . ?"

"Friends?" Jett frowned. "Of course not, Donna, you know that."

"No, Jett." Donna hoped he would catch on. "You know—boys. They get together . . ."

"Donna, we were never together. Harley and I were friends. You've always known that Alex never ran with our crowd. Why are you asking me these questions?" Jett was confused.

"I will be very specific. Jett, when boys are young, sometimes they experiment with other boys once their hormones go wild." Donna could see that Jett was beginning to understand what she was trying to say, but she decided to complete her thought. "At some time in the past did you and Alex have sex?"

"No!" Jett was taken aback by her question. The tone of his voice sounded like he couldn't understand why she would ask such a question. The expression on his face was one of utter shock.

"Okay, then tell me what happened in Green Bay," Donna said.

Donna was asking questions, and that worried Jett. She was confident and well-grounded in her faith, and he had never been able to control her in spiritual matters.

"I haven't told anyone about seeing Alex in Green Bay because I didn't want to upset The Coach. Annie was pregnant with Ben, and it would have been too much for her to handle. After a while I put the whole incident out of my mind." Jett sat down beside her.

"I'll tell you now what happened: The night before Alex Marshall ran off to Atlanta, he came to the team hotel. He managed to get to our floor, and he was using scripture to get into our room for a sexual advance; he always had a thing for me. That night Harley tried to keep me from laying it on the line with Alex. Now he's trying to make me feel guilty."

"What did you say to Alex?" Donna asked.

"I stopped Alex's sexual advance by calling it what it was." Jett was firm, but then he softened. "That's all—nothing more."

"Thanks for telling me," Donna said, cautiously. Her husband had never lied to her, but she sensed she wasn't getting the full story.

"Satisfied?" Jett took her in his arms and held her. He smiled as if he had just asked her to marry him. Donna nodded and returned the smile.

"I need to check on Will," she said.

She started to walk out of the room, but then she turned. Jett was taking off his shoes.

"What?" he asked.

"I forgot to tell you that I offered to bring food to the Whitleys for Annie's first night back."

"You did what?" he yelled.

"I offered to prepare food for Annie's first night back."

"You're preparing food for the man who's made a mockery of God?" The veins stuck out on his neck and his face turned red.

"I'm helping Annie and Wayne," Donna said as she came back to face Jett.

"I can't believe you would offer to help. Do you realize what you've done?"

"It's Alex Marshall's last chance. I—we must offer ourselves to God to be used in this very critical time. If for no other reason, you owe it to The Coach. If Alex is everything you say he is, then you need to work harder in a positive way to win him to the Lord."

"I won't permit you to take food to them!"

Donna stood there for a few seconds before answering. "Fine, I'll do as you ask, but I'm going to pray that God will give you a compassionate heart toward Alex Marshall."

She walked out of the room. Jett waited until she was down the hall before he punched his fist through the wall, and pain shot up his arm. He sat on the bed again as he rubbed it.

"God, I can't tell anyone about what happened when I ignored Alex's message for me," Jett said. "What would people say? What would Donna say?"

He picked up his shoe and threw it across the room.

"If it got out I'd be ruined," Jett muttered. "Just don't remind me anymore of what I did wrong. I'm sorry—okay? Just leave me alone, and I'll be fine."

HAMILTON HOME

Kitty said good-bye to her family and decided to lie down on the sofa in the den before leaving for Green Bay. She was feeling a wave of morning sickness. Today was a turn of events that she'd never have imagined could happen five years ago: Harley trying to get Jett to repent.

Jett had always been the strong one spiritually. He had been her rock when the pain of her marriage cut her to the bone. It had been unbearable for her when Harley was sent back to prison because of a parole violation. The judge didn't care that Harley's little redheaded wife was pregnant or that his dad was Tom Hamilton, the high-powered president of a bank. Harley had sixteen months left on his original sentence, and the judge imposed an additional two years for the half-gram of cocaine found in his pocket.

As usual, Harley was sorry for being caught, but he had come to think his cleverness was bigger than the law. Life was one big party and responsibility was a joke. Their family problems grew steadily each year. Because their parents were best friends, the idea of a divorce was difficult and would put relationships in a precarious position. Finally she saw divorce as her only option.

Six weeks after Harley's return to prison, his father suffered a massive heart attack on Thanksgiving. Tom was Harley's hero, and Tom's love for his son was boundless as well. Jett found the judge at home in the middle of his holiday dinner and appealed to him to give Harley a compassionate furlough. Miraculously it was granted, and within a few hours Harley was released into Jett's custody. They made it to the hospital just minutes before Tom took his last breath.

Tom whispered, "My boy," as he reached to hug his son one last time.

Jett tenderly touched Harley's shoulder and said, "Your dad has been waiting to tell you he loves you."

Harley could not see his father through his tears. "I'll change. I promise. Just don't die, Daddy," Harley begged, but it was too late.

Over the next few days of his leave, Harley realized how much he had thrown away. One daughter told him that he should have been the one to die.

Another wouldn't make eye contact. Kitty's love had grown cold. As Jett picked him up to return him to prison, the magnitude of his selfish life hit him squarely between the eyes.

Tears rolled down Harley's face as he cried.

"Jett, I've ruined my life. How much worse can it get?"

"Only Jesus can change you. I'll do everything in my power to help you resolve the things that you've been so careless with. But you have to take the first step. Honor your dad's love by changing."

They were ready to enter the prison door. Harley was shrouded in dread and despair. Jett was worried he might try something reckless.

"The warden is waiting for you," said a guard. "Let me escort you to his office."

Harley and Jett walked into the office. A look of relief crossed the warden's face.

"I'm so sorry about your father's passing," he said. "Here's your uniform. Go into my restroom and change. I'll take you back to your cell for roll call. We have five minutes."

Harley touched the suit with his fingers and doubled over with great heaves. Jett bent down to help him stand.

"I'll be here on Sunday—just two days away. Okay?" There was no hint of condemnation in Jett's voice.

Jett wanted Harley to know how much he had to live for. He paced beside the warden's desk. Could he say everything that needed to be said in these last few minutes to give Harley hope? But there would be no words, because Jett couldn't speak. The lump in his throat grew when he saw Harley in his prison uniform.

Here was a friend who knew Jett's insecurities: a childhood filled with extreme poverty and academic struggles. Harley had worked to improve Jett's life. He would slip him money, tutor him, or think of a dramatic football play to make Jett the star. If he could, Jett would have given his life to save Harley from this seemingly endless path of personal destruction.

God just needed to give Jett more time, because less than a minute remained. He began to panic, but he knew football games had been won in less time. Surely God could give Jett a word to affect a positive change.

The warden stood. "Harley, we need to go."

Jett walked toward Harley. In his mind he saw Tom Hamilton, and he envisioned the hug he'd give Harley were he here. It was always Tom's way of letting Harley know that he was going to take care of him no matter what. Jett wasn't the type of person to do this, but he knew he had to do something. When Jett reached the trembling Harley, he slipped his hands behind Harley's head and drew him to his chest. His arms encircled Harley, just like Tom had done a thousand times.

Jett wished he could tell Harley what was in his heart—that before he met Harley he had only dreamed of a real friend. Jett's heart broke as the warden took Harley from the room, and he fell prostrate in travail for his friend's soul. The next day Harley gave his life to the Lord, and for the next thirty-eight months Jett worked with him to mentor an effective change. Not only did Harley's heart change, but so did his approach to life.

Kitty never regretted giving Harley another chance. She knew the foundation was laid by the brotherly love that Jett Taylor had for her husband. But in the last couple of weeks, Jett had transitioned to a person who used words to cut at people and hurt them. The change in him was oddly similar to the change her parents had seen in The Coach when Kitty was a child.

Like Alex needed a miracle for his health, Jett needed a miracle for his heart. He needed to be able to love people again. And Kitty began to pray.

SUSAN SPENCER'S HOME

"Sure, Harley, I'll be here all afternoon."

Susan Spencer hung up the telephone. She didn't have to ask Harley why he was coming to visit. She had been thinking about Alex since Wayne made his announcement. Why would Jett oppose Alex coming home to die? So what if Annie and Wayne were permitting his companion to come? It was a kind gesture, and the Whitleys could manage any sort of tension that resulted from the situation.

Susan sat in the living room of her tiny house on the corner by the high school. She had grown up with Alex and Annie's dad. They had even dated, but she married a veteran who had died a few months later in a grain elevator fire. Susan never remarried and had no children. Her niece Kitty was the closest thing she had to a daughter. The McKenzie-Hamilton-Linder families were her only living relatives, and her students and former students like Alex received the love she would have given her own family.

The Bill Marshall she remembered was as handsome as any Hollywood leading man with dark wavy hair and large, deep brown eyes. Every pore appeared to burst with testosterone. Bill was the area's most eligible bachelor, and he had charmed his way into many a girl's heart.

Year later he became known for being brutal with his words and discipline. Even his most athletic football players would collapse under the pressure. In his thirties Bill changed his life, but his spiritual motto was similar to his life creed: "My way or the highway."

Even as he lay dying, The Coach would not change his heart toward Alex. Susan remembered the day she sat by his side talking over times they had shared. As the visit came to a close, Susan spoke gently.

"Give Alex the opportunity to reconcile your relationship before you die, Bill. Just call him."

"The prodigal son made the first move. I wait every day praying he'll come home, but he can't come home and think he's going to sleep with boys in Hallton."

Susan looked around the room. Pictures of football players covered walls and dressers. Trophy footballs and sports awards were mixed among his belongings. There was not one picture of Alex.

"The father of the prodigal son in the Bible never put any conditions on the son. You've inspired a lot of boys. You've been good to Annie and her family, but there are no sufficient words to tell you how horrible you've been to Alex. Won't you consider it? Soon you'll stand before the Living God, and then what will be your excuse for not forgiving Alex?" Susan said.

"I have my son. His name is Jett," The Coach said through his pain.

"You foolish old man, Jett just needed a father figure, and for some reason he chose you. How could you have such a hard heart toward your own son?"

"My son Alex is a faggot. My son Jett is a hero."

"Jett *isn't* your son. You've had too much medication. Listen to me." She pulled his face so he could see her eye-to-eye. "Bill, you can correct all those wrongs if you just repent for the way you treated Alex. What you're doing is a sin."

"Alex deserves to go to hell. Just leave me alone." Bill turned his head, and Susan stood and left.

Within two days Bill Marshall was dead. Though many mourned him for what he contributed to their lives, Susan grieved for what he left undone.

Now she prayed for Alex. "Father, what would you have us do for Alex?"

Susan's prayer was interrupted when Harley opened the screen door. He sat on the ottoman pulled close to her chair. Susan patted his back, because she saw the distressed look in his face.

"I know, I know. Jesus will help us get through this, just like he helped us get through your problems. We have to trust him."

"Alex is going to die. I could have stopped Jett." He looked at her with sad eyes.

"No one could have stopped Jett today," Susan said. "God is giving us another chance to do right by Alex. Jett has a choice to do what is right, just like Bill Marshall had a choice."

"I could have stopped him in Green Bay but chose to run."

"What are you talking about?" She realized there was more than just this morning.

"The night before Alex left, Jett and Alex had a confrontation in Green Bay. I know Jett is scared, and he'll make life miserable for Annie and Wayne once Alex gets here."

Susan thought about what Harley had told her, and then she said, "Alex could have died in Atlanta, but God is bringing him home to give Jett a chance to repent. We must pray hard for God to have his way—and then act on what God tells us to do."

"How will we know?" Harley asked.

"God never tells us the fifth step until we've taken the first four. We need to pray to know the first step." Susan got on her knees beside Harley.

"Father, we come to you to ask that you bring a miracle to the people in Hallton. We ask for Alex's heart to be restored to you. Heal the hurts, and bring forth those things that are hidden."

They did not know for what they had just prayed.

PART THREE

❧ The Confession ❧

*Have mercy on me, O God, according to your unfailing
love; according to your great compassion blot out my transgressions. Wash away all my iniquity and cleanse me
from my sin.*
*For I know my transgressions, and my sin is always
before me.*

Psalm 51:1–3

18

AUSTIN STRAUBEL INTERNATIONAL AIRPORT,
GREEN BAY ∽ WEDNESDAY, JUNE 15

THE PLAN ON HOW to get to Wisconsin took time to work out. Dr. Moss suggested they fly first class. Scott waited until the last minute so he could book a direct morning flight with the fewest passengers. Wayne was meeting them in Harley's van, which could accommodate Alex's wheelchair. It appeared to be the perfect plan.

Once the plane left the tarmac in Atlanta, Scott realized his life would change forever. Hallton would be the actual beginning of his new life without Alex. They had just taken off when he began to worry about what his co-worker had said, and he struggled with that the entire trip.

"Scott, I can't see you leaving good medical attention and your friends for a place that isn't even on the map," Lesley said.

Scott tried to make light of her comments. "Les, it isn't like I'm moving in with them for good. This is short term. I need to trust them."

But with each passing day, Scott realized how much he needed a family. He wanted to continue to trust Annie and her family beyond Alex's death.

"We're approaching Green Bay. Please fasten your seat belts," the voice said over the speaker.

Now that Scott was going to be at the mercy of people he did not know, it caused his stomach to knot. Maybe he had made a mistake about Annie's sincerity. He feared that until Alex's death he would be a pawn in the Whitleys' attempt to win Alex's soul. What would he do if they beat their Bibles and quoted scripture to him?

An airline official came aboard after everyone deplaned to take Alex out in the wheelchair. Annie and Scott walked on either side of Alex until they reached the sidewalk. There stood Wayne and the boys. Wayne was at least a decade older than Annie, but the whole family fit together like a picture from a magazine. Yet, Scott did not want to be deceived by their sweet innocence.

"Uncle Alex," shouted Ben when he saw them. He ran over and hugged Alex's neck and then kissed him on the cheek.

Scott watched every move, trying to see if they were staged or authentic. He was amazed at young Ben's lack of reticence in kissing his diseased uncle. Wayne was lined up behind Ben to hug Alex.

"Welcome to Wisconsin." Brian greeted Scott with a formal handshake. Ben was right behind him in copycat fashion, but with much more vigor.

"My goodness, it feels cool here after being in Atlanta." Annie hugged Wayne while getting Scott's attention. "Wayne, this is Scott."

"Thanks for coming. We hope you'll consider us family." Less eager than his sons, Wayne was still kind as he, too, shook Scott's hand. "The van is over here. We can give Alex a fairly smooth ride back to the farm."

"How does Wisconsin look, Alex?" Annie asked.

"Looks good, sis," Alex replied, with a smile. "I really can't thank you enough, Wayne."

Wayne saw people staring. Knowing the nature of Alex's relationship with Scott, he felt embarrassed to have touched them. Even though God had put this trip together, the next few weeks would be hard to handle if this feeling continued. Wayne prayed for God to break the barrier around his heart.

"Why don't you let Ben ride with me; we'll follow you," Annie said. They'd brought two vehicles in case Alex became sick and someone needed to go for help.

Wayne finished loading the van while Annie got into the car. Her report on Alex's condition had not been adequate preparation. Alex appeared so frail that Wayne feared any bump would break him open like a sand dollar.

"Uncle Alex looks terrible, Mom," Ben said as they left the airport.

Recently he'd found pictures of Alex his mom had saved in an old shoebox. He was in second grade when he met his uncle at The Coach's funeral. Ben remembered when they moved into The Coach's house to take care of him; his grandfather angrily demanded those pictures be burned. Instead, Annie carefully put them out of the old man's sight. On Alex's birthday she would bring the box down from the top shelf and look at them with Ben and his brother.

"Yes, he does." Annie merged into traffic. "How did Dad get a ball out of your hands and the cap off your head to come to the airport?"

Ben was a natural sportsman like his grandfather and was always playing with some sort of ball.

"Threats about losing my video games," Ben replied. "Brian and I are ready for you to be home. Dad is in a bad mood when you're gone."

"He just loses his patience with so many responsibilities," Annie said as she muffled a laugh.

As she pulled out onto the highway back to Hallton, Annie said, "So what's been going on?"

"Mr. Hamilton comes over to help Dad everyday with getting the house ready."

"How thoughtful," Annie said. "Any bad news?"

"Well, Brian got a package in the mail. They wouldn't let me see what it was. He doesn't know who sent it, but Brian was real upset."

Annie racked her brain to figure out what he might have gotten and then decided to change the subject.

"Tell me about your baseball games, kiddo, give me your latest stats . . ."

They talked about ball games until they were home.

FIRST CHURCH, AUSTIN

"Will you see that the courier gets these when he comes this afternoon?" Samuel asked. His possessions were being moved from the church to his home—this was his last day in the office.

"So what are you doing now to make them shake in their boots?" Esther smiled. "You've turned this church upside down."

"I just wanted to start doing what was right. Few people understand that you can be committed to Christ, remain biblical, and address social issues. What frightens me is when I hear them repeat some legalistic gem I've said in the past."

"Most still think this is your plan for getting a specific new wife named Candace."

After Sunday's service the elders met with Samuel to warn him of the eternal damnation he faced if he continued to believe the lies of the devil. Humor helped sustain Samuel and Esther through the negative calls, faxes, and unfriendly visits. Those who supported Samuel were chastised and reprimanded.

"I'll pass on a new wife." Samuel put most of the white envelopes on her desk.

Esther picked up an envelope and asked, "What does this letter say?"

"It's for the elders. I ask forgiveness for being so legalistic, and again I ask them to examine their lives. If the letter touches one heart it will be good."

Samuel pulled a chair close to her desk. Most of the staff was at lunch, and he felt comfortable being in her office. For thirty years Esther had been his rock at work. She had never been a yes-person just because of his position.

"I'd like some man to befriend Brent to help him work through his anger. I've made calls this week, and there are a few who say they will consider it. God has people to fill those roles—if they'll just step out and do it," Samuel said as he fiddled with two other envelopes.

"Do you have any moving instructions?" Esther asked as she looked down to sort the first stack of envelopes.

"I'm leaving in a few minutes, and I won't be here when Gerald goes through my things. I've made space in the garage for the movers to put everything there."

Neither of them commented on this odd turn of events. Eubanks had sent word through his secretary that before any boxes were moved he would personally make sure there was nothing taken that belonged to the church. His unspoken accusation was that Samuel had come to the church with just a Bible in his hands and had purchased every text and trinket with church funds. It was just another bogus attempt to make Samuel feel poorly about the recent decisions he had made.

Samuel hesitated as he handed Esther one of the remaining envelopes. "Is something the matter?" she asked.

"Not really—just another step in the process of taking the things that belonged to the one you love and . . ." Samuel decided to continue in a more positive manner than to discuss the sting of slowly eliminating the loved one's presence from the home. Surely Natalie would be exuberant over what Samuel was doing with her possessions.

"I've sold Natalie's car. Enclosed is a check from the sale. I want you and your husband to help people in need. Candace might need financial assistance once she leaves the shelter. It wouldn't be proper for a widower to give money to a married woman. I'd like to be the silent partner and count on you two as the administrators. Deal?"

"Deal. This is an answer to a prayer," said Esther. "We were just talking last night about how to do something like that."

"Excellent. As well, I plan to begin packing her clothes and various personal items—maybe some household items as well that can be used for women who move quickly and need—uh—something." Samuel smiled. "Natalie would have wanted it that way."

"Yes, she would have," Esther replied. It appeared that Samuel was beginning to give from the depth of his being. She knew that these steps were difficult.

Samuel handed her the last envelope. His words were thick with pain.

"This one is for Scott. After I leave the country, please FedEx it to him. It details his mother's death. Enclosed is a house key if he'd like to collect any personal effects. I've told him that he can smash everything that belongs to me. The address of his new office is on the envelope. The phone number is the same. They've just moved a few blocks."

"How do you know something like that?" Esther smiled.

"You know very well I drive by his office whenever I'm in Atlanta." Samuel could not meet her eyes. "Sometimes I sit outside just to catch a glimpse of him."

"Why didn't you ever go inside? Honestly, Samuel, he could be as scared as you about making the first contact."

Samuel looked at his gray suit pants and ran his finger along the fine stripe. His repentance was real, but contacting Scott was just too difficult for him.

"I'm taking the coward's way out by sending him a letter instead of speaking to him in person." A hint of tears came to his eyes. "I'm afraid of his rejection."

"Samuel, God can give you the courage to face Scott. Prayer works wonders," Esther said with a smile as she handed him a tissue.

"I know it does, but it's been a long time since I allowed God to open the doors in his time," Samuel said, wiping his eyes.

"Being an 'ex' preacher living under a cloud of suspicion sort of limits the number of people who'll make things work out for you. Am I right?" Esther had a way of saying things that got him to smile.

"You know me too well. I've got a date for prayer today."

"Going to see Natalie?" Esther asked, knowing that in recent days he almost lived by her grave.

Samuel picked up a pen from her desk and began doodling on a Post-it as he answered. "Actually, no; I'm going to see Miss Lois and her little prayer group. It's time I start being with people who truly have God's attention."

Samuel smiled and then continued to speak of this elderly woman in the congregation.

"It's real funny: for years I've preached about God blessing us with tangible things so onlookers would say, 'Man, God gives him miracles—I need to become a Christian.' As well, I could always count on my high-powered business or church connections to work out my needs. But when I got down to the bottom and thought about seeking out someone who knew the heart of God—anyone, anywhere—Miss Lois was the only person I knew who had an open door to him."

Samuel then added, "I've already met with them once, and we're praying for Scott—not to come home, but for him to truly know that Jesus loves him."

"That is a prayer that will be answered," Esther said.

19

WHITLEY HOME ~ WEDNESDAY AFTERNOON

"WE'RE HOME." Wayne pulled into the gravel driveway with potholes that had been there since Alex was a child. He drove the van directly up to the front of the steps.

"There's Harley," he commented as Harley came out of the house. Seeing an anxious look cross Alex's face, Wayne added, "Harley isn't a nauseating macho man now that he's a Christian."

"I'm happy for him," Alex mumbled.

Harley carried Alex into the house and took him to the bedroom that had belonged to The Coach. Painful childhood memories inundated Alex as soon as he entered the house. In the living room he avoided the scornful eye of his father's ghost. He used to hide in the corner closet and cry longingly for his mother's arms around him.

The smells of the countryside were pleasant. The crisp white room was inviting. A hospital bed was next to the large window overlooking the yard where Alex had played as a child. He could see the traffic coming from Hallton. Mirrors had been removed so Alex would not reflect on his physical appearance. A daybed with a pillow and blanket was next to Alex's bed so someone else could sleep in the room with him.

Harley laid Alex on the bed and Annie began to make him comfortable.

"Let me go help unload the van. Kitty will be here soon to check on you," Harley said to him. Turning to leave, he looked back at Alex. "I'm glad you came home."

Alex managed a weak smile before Harley left. Annie walked out of the bedroom carrying some of Alex's medications that needed to be refrigerated.

"Looks like they're coming down the driveway now," Wayne said. He was standing in the middle of the living room gazing out the large set of double windows.

"Who?" Annie asked as she walked toward the kitchen. A stack of mail caught her attention. Putting down the meds she flipped through it.

"Kitty and Susan are bringing food." Wayne walked over to open the door.

Annie opened an envelope. She read a few lines and ran her fingers through her hair and then tore it into small pieces and placed it deep within a garbage bag. Kitty and Susan entered the house with their hands full of medical paraphernalia and food.

"The timing is perfect." Annie hugged them.

"Welcome home," Kitty said. "How's Alex doing?"

"Real well, actually. This has been a smooth transition compared to when he came home from the hospital two weeks ago. I'm encouraged," Annie said.

"Dr. Moss felt that you being in Atlanta made all the difference. He said the improvements Alex made were nothing short of miraculous." Kitty put down her medical bag. "Where is he?"

"In The Coach's old room." Annie turned to Susan. "Thanks for all you've done."

"There's more in the car. Where's Harley when I need him?" Susan asked.

"He went to the workshop with Brian. They'll be coming right through this room any minute. Kitty, come with me," Annie said.

Kitty followed her into Alex's room. Ben closed the suitcase he was unpacking.

"Welcome home, Alex." Kitty went to the bed to greet him.

"Good to see you," Alex replied, returning her hug.

"Dr. Moss took great pains in making sure this trip would be smooth. Alex has handled it very well," Annie said.

"Let me give you a little checkup, and then you need to rest." Kitty gave a little inquiring nod to see if it was okay to begin. When Alex returned it with a smile she gently put the stethoscope on Alex's chest and spoke quietly so only he could hear.

"I never thought you'd be at the other end of my stethoscope. This is my first official case of AIDS in Hallton, but I'm not a novice. When we lived in New York in the early '80s I had some AIDS patients. Confidentially, I currently have several patients who are HIV-positive. People in Hallton would be scandalized if they knew—they think that stuff like this only happens in the city." Kitty sounded confident when she added, "But I'll take good care of you. Whatever I'm not sure of, I have colleagues all the way to Chicago who can give me direction."

"Thanks, Kitty. I'm lucky to have you." Alex was drained after being active for so many hours.

Scott came in from putting his suitcases and equipment into the room that adjoined Alex's room.

"I'd like you to meet Scott," Alex said. Kitty turned and shook his hand.

"I'm Kitty Hamilton—we've talked on the phone. We're glad to have you in Hallton. I believe you've already met my husband."

"Yes, I have." Scott smiled.

Annie motioned for Scott and they left the room. Kitty turned back to Alex and listened to his heart, which sounded good. She took his blood pressure and pulse. As she was looking into Alex's mouth, the door opened.

"Need another hand?" Harley asked.

"Sweetie, give me another five minutes and, Harley, don't eat up all the food. Remember it belongs to the Whitleys." Kitty laughed her famous laugh and smiled her beautiful smile.

Harley smiled at her like he had from across the room in school. Alex always sat next to Kitty in a class that used alphabetical seating, and he witnessed their looks of love. Alex recalled that they had included him in their twosome in chemistry class. Harley had entertained them with his hilarious stories each morning.

Kitty turned to Alex. "I can't feed that boy enough now that he's back to home cooking."

Scott walked into the room with Alex's squeeze water bottle. He put it down on the table and then turned to leave.

"Please stay, Scott. I'll need your help maneuvering Alex." Kitty checked the muscle tone in Alex's limbs. "We've had a great deal happen since you left. When your dad died, Harley was in prison and I had gone to visit him the weekend of the funeral. Did you know he was in prison, Alex?"

"The sports section was never my favorite." Alex relaxed a little. "I vaguely remember someone saying Harley was in prison, but it never registered. How long did he stay? What were the charges?"

"Several things—he'll tell you. It's truly a miracle our family is together." Kitty continued her examination. "I want you to roll toward me, and Scott will assist. Roll on three: one, two, and three."

"How do you think I'm doing?"

"Great for a man who is as sick as you've been lately, but all of you Marshalls are fighters. I don't see why you won't be around for a while." Kitty smiled. "Please talk to my husband, Alex. He's been waiting for you like a kid at Christmas. It won't hurt, I promise. He just wants to repent." Kitty left to get Harley.

Scott waited until he knew they were alone before asking, "Why does he need to repent? Did Harley hurt you?"

"Not really," Alex said. His stomach knotted up as Harley entered.

"Kitty tells me I have five minutes. May I talk?" Harley pulled the cane chair over to the bed.

☙ ☙ ☙

Annie and Wayne went to the porch to get some alone time together. Susan insisted they get out of the house while she put groceries away and prepared the table for a meal.

"I've missed you so much, Wayne."

"There's no one who can replace you." Wayne let out a sigh of satisfaction. "I don't know how you do it."

"Ben told me they're glad I'm home."

Wayne laughed. "I wish I could harness his energy and sell it."

"Well, let's hope there'll be a payoff somewhere along the way with a college scholarship or a major-league contract." Annie changed her tone. "What happened with Brian?"

"Someone sent him a box of condoms and a lewd note about Alex and Scott. Ben wasn't supposed to say anything."

"I coerced it out of him," she said. "Why didn't you tell me what you've been through?"

"You had other things to think about. I expected a negative backlash after the way Jett acted in church—word spreads like a wildfire in this town." Wayne sank his teeth into an apple he had grabbed on the way outside.

Annie looked across the countryside. "Jett can be a caring man, but he needs to learn more about grace."

"That's a kind way of looking at it, honey." Wayne sat down beside her in the swing. "I'd like about ten minutes with Jett in a dark alley."

"What did he say?"

"Start with 'blasphemers of God' and 'unrepentant sodomites.'"

"Then that would explain the note," she said.

"What note?" Wayne stopped swinging and looked at her.

"I got a little note of condemnation from Janet Linder. She used those exact words."

"The last of the Linders to have their say: it started with Paul after church."

"Paul? I wouldn't have guessed him. He's been your best friend since you could talk."

"Well, you never know about people. Even if Alex never says anything about Jesus, I'm satisfied we've done the right thing."

"Me too," Annie smiled at him. "What do you think of Scott?"

"He's a nice man," Wayne said with a bit of hesitation.

"Tell me the truth. Does it bother you having him here?"

"It's me, not Scott. When I saw the stares of people at the airport I realized how deep this has gotten, and I can't get beyond their relationship. I'd like to be more demonstrative, but I'm really repulsed. Annie, I can't believe this has happened. I thought I was ready, but I'm not."

"Do you doubt that we should have asked Scott here?" Annie asked.

Wayne shook his head. "No, I know God wants them both here. I've got to go on faith and not on feelings. God will change my heart." Wayne held her hand. "I think I'll give Clark a call to tell him you're home. Maybe we can meet this evening to discuss the guys being here."

"Good idea. God worked out my feelings; I know he'll do the same for you."

They sat in the swing and enjoyed the moment.

❧ ❧ ❧

Scott felt he should allow Alex and Harley some privacy, and he made an excuse to leave. "I need something to drink. Want anything?" Scott said as he headed for the door.

Harley shook his head. As Scott closed the door, Harley turned to Alex.

"I really don't know how to say . . ." Harley's heart pounded as he paused to gather the words he needed. "I'm sorry for not helping you."

"No need to be sorry. Jett was right."

"I don't know what Jett said, but it hurt you. I'm sorry for not staying there to defend you."

"You don't know? I always just assumed you knew . . ." The last sentence was barely audible. Harley let Alex's comment slip past him, because he wanted so desperately to befriend Alex.

"Alex, I don't know exactly where to begin. I know we didn't ever hang out or talk and I regret that. It's been a long time. I'll start with college. We all went to the University of Alabama. Kitty and I married our second year in college, just like we'd always planned. Our twin girls, though, were a surprise and were born just after graduation. Kitty got accepted to medical school in Chicago, and I got drafted by the Giants in New York.

"I was out for myself for a good many years. It started when I couldn't handle the popularity. Too many people wanted to be my friend, but for all the wrong reasons: money, sex. From there—you know what happened, don't you?"

"I'm told you went to prison. I wish you'd called me to defend you."

"Why would you want to defend me?" Harley asked.

"You needed my help." Alex remembered the offer from Harley to walk him to the car that fateful night. "You're my friend."

Harley grabbed Alex's hand.

"You were a friend to me, but I was never a real friend to you. I'm so sorry." Harley would not let his eyes meet Alex's as he spoke.

"So why did you go to prison?" Alex was gentle.

"In the fall of 1987 I started betting on my own games—it was my ninth year of professional ball and I wasn't raking it in like I used to. The Feds began collecting evidence at the year's end. Mid-season in 1988 they set me up with someone who was wired. When I cut the deal with prosecutors I thought old Harley would be able to make it."

"What was the deal?"

"Lifetime ban from professional sports. Persona non grata of the NFL. I'm sort of *The Man without a Country* of professional football: they don't recognize me, and I'm to forget them."

"I forgot how you have a way with words," Alex smiled. "But I'm thinking of your *other* sentence—what was it?"

"Two years in prison. But I knew I could pretend I had changed and be paroled in eight months. Everything was always a game with me; I know you remember that. It's no game now to realize how many doors are slammed in my face because of my prison record," Harley said with regret.

Alex nodded, and he felt sorry for his former adversary.

"After I was released for good behavior I started doing the same things again. I got caught violating my parole—it was a police sting on an illegal gambling establishment. This time I had cocaine on me, and that added to my sentence. I ended up serving forty months the second time. When my dad died I knew I had to change."

"I'm sorry to hear about your father. So how did you change?"

Harley smiled. "I never made a real decision for Christ until three years ago. When I gave God control of my life, my life started changing. For one, I'm clean from all substances."

"Congratulations," Scott said, coming into the room and seating himself on the sofa.

"Thanks. All this is to say I'm sorry that I wasn't more effective in stopping—that mess." Harley kept it vague so that only Alex would understand.

"No regrets. I'm really tired, but if you come back another day, I'd like to talk some more."

Alex held out his right hand to Harley. It was met with a hug.

"I'll be back." Harley turned to shake Scott's hand and left.

"What was all that?" Scott asked.

"He apologized for not helping me—uh, back in high school. He's gotten religion, that's all."

"He seems nice. Do you think we'll get a lot of proselytizing like that while we're here?"

"A little, I'd imagine. I expect Susan—that's Kitty's aunt and my old teacher—will say something about my need to trust Jesus, but you're the only one who's never let me down," Alex said. "He really isn't like they promised."

"Who? Harley?"

"No—Jesus; we were promised that nothing would be the same once we got Jesus in our lives," Alex mumbled to himself.

"What? I can't understand you," Scott urged.

Alex spoke louder. "None of us got what we were promised. Jesus was supposed to be so good."

Scott understood. He would rather not think about trusting Jesus, because trusting Annie was all he could handle.

FIRST CHURCH, AUSTIN ✦ THAT EVENING

The atmosphere wasn't light in this unplanned meeting of the leadership of Austin First Church. There was a strain among the men who governed this Christian body. They were dedicated, and everything they did was what they thought God was calling them to do. A good number opposed Samuel's decision to help Candace, but there were a few others who applauded his steps to protect her. However, all of them were unhappy about Samuel's sudden resignation when he had breakfast with Gerald Eubanks. Many had even ventured to query Eubanks about that morning and why he hadn't done more to stop Samuel from resigning.

Most church members were still in the fellowship hall eating the meal the church provided. It was just twenty minutes before the Wednesday evening service was to begin when Gerald Eubanks called the meeting to order in his office.

"Gentlemen, I wanted to touch base with everyone tonight. Samuel Phillips is completely out of the building. I know this has been an extremely swift move, but the pace of his departure was entirely Samuel's decision. A new era has begun here in Austin. We've already had several men inquire about the senior pastor position, and I'll be passing along résumés in the next few weeks."

Gerald gave a little nod when the door opened and Brent Cooley walked in. Brent had heard the rumors that there was some kind of division within this group of men. He intended to have his wife back before July, but that would only happen if these men helped him. Ordinarily there wouldn't be a rush, but Brent wanted to make sure that before Samuel went to Peru, he would know that Brent had won.

Gerald stood and greeted Brent with a handshake.

"I've asked Brent to come tonight to say a few words. Our time is short, and he will limit his remarks." Gerald then offered his chair to Brent.

"I'm humbled by you, my brothers. You've recognized that Samuel's intentions weren't honorable toward my wife, and with a swift sword you've removed the albatross."

A few eyes shifted and voices cleared. There was a noticeable wave of unrest. Everyone was thinking that Brent's words were a bit strong.

"I'm not a perfect man. I lost my temper with my wife, but haven't we all at one time or another? Today's world is a difficult place to work in when you're a committed Christian. There's a great deal of stress in being the biblical head of the family, working a full day, paying the bills, and then making time for the family's needs. It's stressful, isn't it? I can see you understand by the looks on your faces.

"There's no one here who can cast any stone at me for having a flash of anger when my wife overspent our funds on something foolish. My weak moment was followed by a humble apology. However, I know that the Lord keeps forgiving, and I'm moving forward."

The foolish spending Brent spoke of was the wrong brand of potato chips, with a cost difference of a few cents.

"I'm asking you—my dear friends and partners in this wonderful church—to help me find my wife and encourage her to come home. Our marriage cannot be saved with her away from our home. I've told Gerald that I will sit under his leadership and learn how to be a better husband."

Brent swallowed as if he were holding back tears. This speech had been rehearsed all day.

"I know that the evening service will begin in just minutes, but I can talk with you afterwards. I love my family so much, and for me to be a better husband, I must have my wife at home. Don't you agree, gentlemen?" Brent opened his arms wide toward them. "Wouldn't you want me to do all that was within my power if the tables were turned and your wife was living out of the home?"

Brent then looked at his watch.

"I know I have to let you get back to your duties as leaders of the greatest church in this area—you're my leaders, leading me each day to a more perfect relationship with my Savior and Lord."

His words were like a vapor, mesmerizing unsuspecting, good men into his web of lies. There would be no after-service talk, because Brent had scheduled a business dinner away from the church. Brent intended to have things his way.

CLARK'S OFFICE ~ WEDNESDAY NIGHT

"Come in, Wayne."

Clark stood up from his desk and offered Wayne a seat.

"Thanks for seeing me on such short notice. I know this is a busy day," Wayne began before he settled on the sofa. "I really don't know what to do. I'm having a hard time dealing with Alex and Scott's relationship."

"Are they being demonstrative?"

"No. I've seen less affection pass between them than I see on Sunday when we're all hugging each other. Yet, when I was at the airport, I felt so strange. People were staring."

Clark nodded and said, "You're doing what God called you to do. John 13 says for us to love one another just as he loved us—without conditions—but it isn't easy, is it?"

"I want to relate to Scott, but I've got a wall around my heart that keeps me from being genuinely warm to him. Alex is my brother-in-law; I don't think of him as gay."

"I've been studying what the Bible says about manhood," Clark said. "Our view of man's role is based on social norms and not the Word of God."

"I can see that; go on—tell me more," Wayne said.

"Relating to someone who's gay can be very hard, but the bottom-line reason is ridiculous. Homosexuality is threatening, because as men, our sexuality is what affirms us. Of course, sexuality isn't what makes us men at all. If it was, then those men who shave twice a day, have bulging biceps, and have sex with scores of women would be the real men. You know that isn't God's definition. A real man validates another man in the middle of a personal storm. Scott is like you or me. The reason he's a homosexual isn't our concern. Scott needs to be affirmed as a man for his godly qualities."

"Scott's a nice man, but that still doesn't help me with my feelings," Wayne said.

"Take your time. Being Scott's friend won't hurt you as a Christian, as a heterosexual, or in any way I can think of. So what if people talk? People can turn on you in an instant. If people question why you're taking a gay man to coffee, let them think whatever they want. Let God deal with them; can you do that?"

"I'll try," Wayne said slowly. He thought a moment before he said, "How is this so easy for you, Clark?"

"Trial by fire, Wayne, it's just what you're going through now. There was a time when I was similar to your father-in-law. Then I had a personal crisis with my daughter and had to rethink my life: living the way Jesus taught or just speaking hollow words from a pulpit. I don't discuss it openly because we're still in the middle of healing our hurts. I'd appreciate you keeping this confidential."

"Oh yes, I certainly will. Thanks for your support through all of this," Wayne said.

"Wayne, you've got the heart of a peacemaker. You encouraged Annie to make the trip to Atlanta to make peace for the family. You've brought Alex home so he can make peace with the community. With that in mind let me throw this in for your consideration: everything Jesus did was spiritual. When it comes to peacemaking, think of it in the spiritual realm. A peacemaker is one who can bring peace to another man's heart. What you're doing right now is bringing peace to Alex's heart. By being Scott's friend you'll bring him peace, also. Think about it: Scott trusts you and Annie enough to uproot his business and come to an unknown place. In part it has to do with Alex, but he also knows he can depend on you and your family."

"It has to be the spirit of the Lord drawing him," Wayne was quick to say.

"It's more than that, Wayne. Atlanta is full of Christians, but he picked you all. You're the same family that didn't want him to come up for The Coach's funeral, but now he trusts you to honor his relationship with Alex until Alex passes away. I've read that some families come in at the last minute and throw out the partner. Think of the opportunity they're missing."

"To witness to them, is that what you mean? I've thought about doing that already," Wayne replied.

"No, Wayne. When you get down to a person who has a loved one who's dying—they don't want to hear about Acts, Romans, or Psalms. They want to have people meet them in the middle of their grief and help with their pain. God is using you. Who knows what else God will be able to do with your simple acts of selfless love?"

Clark smiled and then stopped and considered the question before he asked, "By the way, has Jett called?"

"I doubt if he'll call while Alex is alive," Wayne said, with a sigh.

"Remember how out of balance your father-in-law was. Jett is becoming a carbon copy of The Coach. When you get worried about what people think, just remember that Jesus would be doing exactly as you are doing. He'd have Scott and Alex in his home. Let's pray right now."

20

CHRISTIAN WOMEN'S CLUB MEETING
JUNE 1, 2007

"As FRIENDS CAME TO VISIT, we could see God's hand changing Alex and Scott." Annie continued her talk. "You see, people—mostly Christians—had hurt them, and it took the love of Christians to begin the restoration process.

"As the days went by, Harley and Alex bonded. They were able to laugh and trade stories. It was almost as if Harley was putting back together the pieces of Alex's soul that had been ripped out over the years. There was one day, however, that was pivotal to the rest of Alex's time on Earth. Because of this, God was able to work many miracles in Alex as well as Scott."

WHITLEY HOME FRIDAY, JUNE 24, 1994

"Scott, the legend goes something like this: Harley was working at football practice with the incoming ninth grade football players. As a joke he hid the ball, and as usual . . ." Alex looked at Harley. "Is that right: as usual?"

"*All the time* is more like it." Harley shook his head with a quick look of disgust that quickly turned into a huge smile.

"Okay, all the time The Coach would single Harley out and use his standard form of coach-discipline. On this particular day, I figure, he wanted to make these new, little guys shiver in their boots, so he . . ." Alex started laughing.

Harley picked up the story.

"Okay, Scott, it really is this simple. The Coach was known for taking a one-by-four piece of wood to anyone who did anything wrong. When it came my time to 'meet him in his office' The Coach always had this little snarling comment: see if you laugh about this. Well, that day I decided I would laugh."

Scott's eyes grew wide, his mouth dropped, and he shook his head as if he couldn't believe anyone would do such a thing. During his short stay in Hallton, Scott had already heard many uncomplimentary stories about The Coach. Crossing the man sounded like a foolish thing to do.

"Instead of it ending there, The Coach up and calls my father who was in a director's meeting at the bank. It just happened to be the worst one he ever had with that group of old codgers. Daddy came to the school for fifteen of the longest minutes of my life and completely finished what The Coach started."

Everyone burst out with another peel of side-splitting laughter.

"That story isn't that funny for me." Harley then added, "Scott, I want to be fair about it. Daddy only paddled me a couple of times after I was eight years old. This was a very unusual reaction, because his typical punishment was yard work."

"They had the best-looking yard in the county," Alex joked. "Didn't Harley's work put the house on the tour of homes?"

"I know that every year they were on the tour people would come all the way out here from Green Bay just to look at that immaculate yard," Calvin replied.

Alex highly regarded Dr. Calvin Johnson, another old friend who had come with Harley for a morning visit. He was a chemistry teacher at the high school and pastor of a large, predominantly African American church. His parents were sharecroppers on The Coach's land, so Calvin and Alex had been neighbors growing up.

"We all thought there was nothing in there. Scott, this experience is better known as: the epitome of stupidity." Calvin knocked on Harley's head like it was a piece of wood. "People say Harley sounded like a cat with his tail caught in the door once his daddy got hold of him in that locker room."

Annie walked into the room and smiled. "Are you talking about the time Harley laughed at The Coach? I heard they gave Harley some kind of award at the class reunion, like 'Providing the Best School Memory.'"

With everyone laughing—including Annie and a couple of the school jocks—Alex finally felt accepted. He had wished for this all his life. It had also been good for him to remember that The Coach's second most successful player also knew the man's sadistic side. It was common knowledge that Harley was the school scapegoat when The Coach wanted to make an example of someone.

"Harley, The Coach sure felt his oats about this one," Alex said, "that is, until your mom showed up at school and put a kink in his tail."

"My mom?" Harley asked. "Oh, no, no, no. While Dad was the more patient parent on a daily basis, when I created a problem outside the house, he was the disciplinarian. She'd never come to the school. Trust me, it was always him."

"I think The Coach wanted to discredit your father's childrearing abilities in front of the townspeople. It all changed after your mom paid him a visit," Alex said.

"She did?"

"That night—the evening after she had gone to see him at school—The Coach kept muttering to himself something like, 'Says she'll tell him.' I'd only hear him grumble as he walked around the house," Alex said. "Whatever she had to say, it scared The Coach."

"The Coach was scared of Mom?" Harley's heart was warmed. "Well, he left me alone for the rest of the school year. I was very grateful for that."

"That reminds me, I overheard The Coach saying something ugly about your gambling problems to your mom once, Harley," Calvin said. "Ella said something like, 'I'll tell him everything and you'll die in disgrace.' I thought it was odd at the time, especially when The Coach got away from her as quick as greased lightning."

"What would Mom know about The Coach?" Harley wondered aloud.

Alex was quiet. Years before, he had learned what Ella Hamilton knew about The Coach. Would he ever be able to share the secret with the one who deserved to know the most?

"Thanks for telling me about my mom. When I was in prison she gave up on me, and maybe we can mend our relationship after all."

Alex felt the mood could use a little lightening.

"Cal, I forgot to tell you that my first client paid me with fried chicken, collard greens, macaroni and cheese, and corn bread."

"Now you're talking. I could throw-down on that," Calvin said.

"I could throw up when you start talking about Southern cooking," Harley laughed as he stood. "Look guys, I need to go pick up my girls. Scott, I've found that article I was telling you about. It's in the van. Want to walk outside with me?"

Scott nodded, and soon he was out of the room behind Harley.

Calvin moved closer to Alex's bed.

"Man, I'm glad you're home, Alex." Calvin said. "I'd have been here sooner, but we were on vacation."

"I'm relieved you could make it by before . . ." Alex didn't want to finish the sentence.

"Alex, if there's anything I can do to help while you're here, please tell me." Calvin hesitated, but continued, "You know, we've all had our moments of heartache. I understand things better now that I'm older. I have a clearer picture of our growing-up years. I just wanted to say that as Christians we need to stick together when the times get rough."

"What are you saying?" Alex asked. "As smart as you are, do you really believe that fundamentalist propaganda?"

"It's not propaganda; it's true. If I was part of that hurt you experienced here, please forgive me. The Coach rejected you—everyone knows that. He was a terrible father. If I could, I would heal your hurt, but only Jesus can do that."

"I have no hurt," Alex snapped. "And if this is about Scott and my orientation . . ."

"This isn't about Scott. I think your pain started right here in Hallton," Calvin said. "Alex, please get it resolved. Jesus isn't a myth. He's more alive than we are, and he'll see you through it." Calvin was about to get up, but he decided to take the pressure off Alex.

"You know Harley hasn't been home very long. People around here still blame him for his father's death—for the shame and stress he brought Tom by going back to prison. Did you know Harley can't go to Brodie's Diner because Mr. Brodie said, 'Killers aren't allowed'; we're trying to be there for Harley as he walks through the pain. I want to be there for you, also."

Alex was about to say something when Calvin hugged him and was out of the room. This stately, intelligent African American man seemed to sense his need to make peace—a need greater than Alex wanted to admit.

Questions began to flood Alex's mind: *What do I have to do to be freed from the hurt? Cal said it had nothing to do with Scott. However, most Christians would say Scott was the first thing that had to go.*

Scott opened the door from the adjoining room.

"Did you hear him?" Alex asked.

"Every word. Does what he says mean anything to you other than the obvious? Your problems did begin here, but was there more?"

"I've lived my life with disappointment. I can't say that one incident was any different from the others." Alex looked out the window hoping to catch a last glimpse of Harley and Calvin driving down the road.

Scott quaked inside. He knew Alex needed to pursue what Calvin said, if it was true.

"Alex, I have questions from my past, but I've got time to get answers. Your time is short. Do whatever it takes to make peace with God, and with man."

"What if Cal is wrong?" Alex asked.

"Nothing is lost." Scott said. "Start with why you left."

"Well, there is one incident. But it happened because I was wrong about something," Alex argued.

"One little incident? Whatever it was drove you away from your family and home. Get it reconciled no matter what the price."

Scott understood reconciliation with God. He did not want to stand in Alex's way as the days grew short. This was what he had feared would happen when they came to Hallton.

Alex looked out the window.

What do I need to do to reconcile with Jett?

Jett had not called. Alex had heard his family whisper, but no one said Jett's name in his presence. Alex's time on Earth was almost finished. The choice was Alex's, and whatever was to be done had to be done soon.

21

JETT'S BUSINESS OFFICE ∽ TUESDAY, JUNE 28

THE DOOR OPENED to Jett's luxurious office. In addition to his church duties, Jett owned a line of sports stores. Clark never dropped by uninvited. Even though he felt it was an irritating imposition, Jett maintained his composure.

"Please, sit down." Jett went behind his desk so Clark would not observe any movements that might give away his annoyance. "So what brings you to Green Bay?"

"Hospital visits. As I passed this office park, I realized where I was and decided to drop by."

"I wish you'd called first. We're extremely busy getting ready for fall and we have orders to fill." Jett smoothed his hair.

"I never thought of you as the order-taker sort," Clark said, dryly. "I've been by the Whitleys every day and they haven't heard from you. When are you going to call on them?"

"After Alex dies I'll talk with them about the delusion they've been under and what it's done to them spiritually," Jett replied.

"You're the one who's deluded. I don't know where the problem lies, but this vendetta has to end. I saw it in you when Annie and Wayne first came to us about Alex's sickness, but I think it began long before that," Clark said.

"All Alex's life he's gotten away with things. He'd whine and cry, and Annie would come wipe his nose. Now she's rescuing him again. No one else had the guts to say that Alex has gotten his just desserts. He deserves to die because of his sin." Jett took a deep breath and let out a frustrated sigh. "I see you don't agree with me, so our conversation has come to a close."

Jett stood. Clark remained seated.

"Over the last few weeks I've become well-versed on Alex's past in Hallton. I've also gotten a clearer picture of The Coach. Annie and Wayne are doing a wonderful job in this delicate situation. Jett, it comes down to the one thing that sets Christianity apart from every other religion: grace. It's something that isn't earned—a gift you don't deserve. Our gospel says when Jesus died for our sins he did it out of love for us, a love we didn't earn or deserve."

"I know what grace is." Jett was disgusted at Clark's condescension, and his voice betrayed him. "The Coach was a wonderful man who loved the Lord."

"For whatever reason The Coach didn't understand or practice grace," Clark said. "Quite frankly, Jett, you're following in The Coach's footsteps."

"Alex has entered into an unholy covenant with another man. AIDS is God's judgment."

Clark stood and looked Jett in the eye. "AIDS *isn't* God's judgment. Alex may have made a bad choice that led him to acquiring this virus, but we've all made poor choices."

"Not like Alex," Jett snarled.

"You're making a choice that you'll regret," Clark said with concern.

"I doubt it."

"I venture to say you've made mistakes. No man is without that moment in time when he cries out to God to save him from a hopeless situation. Remember that as you continue to cast shame on Alex Marshall's name."

"Alex has brought about his own shame and shame on his family."

Clark stared at Jett. "We've all sinned—that's what the Bible says. Therefore consider the grace God gives you, and see if you can offer it to Alex."

"So what do you suggest? That I forgive him for ruining his life and those of his family?" Jett asked. "Alex isn't sorry for anything he's done."

"I suggest you ask Alex to forgive you for not being his friend during the hardest battle he's ever had to fight. Ask forgiveness for not supporting him when his father ridiculed him."

"Yeah, right, I've done nothing to ask forgiveness from the likes of him."

"The Bible says if we have an issue against our brother we must reconcile it," Clark said. "When Jesus died for our sins, he spanned the great divide between God and us. Jesus became the connection between man and God; that link is forgiveness. You could be a tool in the healing of Alex's heart if you go to him and ask his forgiveness for yourself and The Coach."

"I can't believe the words coming from your mouth," Jett said.

Clark followed Jett to the door. "Have you ever been to a fox hunt?"

"What?" Jett looked confused.

"You know how the dog chases the fox everywhere it goes? Well, that's how God operates. God will do everything he can to get to Alex before he dies. The only operative that can block God is free will."

"Alex has chosen not to repent. It's his free will that's getting in the way."

"That's true, but wouldn't it be nice when Alex hears Jesus' name spoken that he has a picture of the selfless acts of grace from Christians like you? And then . . ." Clark stopped for a minute before he continued, "he'll be able to cry out for God's mercy because he knew you cared. Think about it."

Clark tapped the lapel of Jett's suit coat and then looked him squarely in the eye. "Could it be that God is chasing you, too?"

Clark left without looking back. Jett shook his head and repeatedly smoothed his hair. He was tired of people telling him what to do. Alex needed to die to show people that God brings judgment to Christians who stray. It had to be true. The Coach had always told him that grace was something earned through a spotless life.

God chasing me? For what? He asked himself.

Jett had paid dearly for his mistake with Rita, and he would never be put in a position again of having to cry out to God for mercy.

❧ ❧ ❧

"Donna, when do you expect him home?" Harley asked. He was on the phone in Kitty's office while she was with a patient in her examination room next door.

"By supper, Harley. I've been giving him the messages. Hasn't he returned your calls?"

"I've left messages all over town. So here it is: Alex is dying. That's my only message."

Harley returned the phone to its cradle. Kitty had come in and was staring at him.

"Don't worry so much about Jett's problems. He'll have to live with himself the rest of his life." Kitty walked over and ran her fingers through his hair before kissing his forehead. "Let God work this one out, okay?"

"It isn't easy. I just want Jett to see Alex. Is that too much to ask?" Harley sat down in the chair.

"It is to someone who doesn't want to face what he's done to another person," Kitty said. "Get your mind off this. Why don't you see if the Whitleys need another set of hands? Page me if Alex gets any worse. He really needs to be hospitalized, but I'm keeping him at home as long as possible to see if he'll rally one more time."

Kitty grabbed a chart off the desk, kissed Harley again, and went back into the examination room. She was surprised to see her cousin.

"You're not Mrs. Kendrick." Kitty smiled as she tossed the chart on the desk and sat down. "Good to see you."

"I asked your nurse to let me surprise you." Janet twirled her bobbed hair under her left ear.

"Why not call? I wouldn't have put you off," Kitty replied rather sadly, knowing this was not a friendly visit.

"I've been there for you through thick and thin, but I can't go with you on this one," Janet said. "Remember, I convinced your mom and dad to forgive Harley."

"Yes, I do. Why not do it for the Whitleys, also?" Kitty asked.

"Why are you helping Alex? Don't you know you could get AIDS? Alex has done a terrible thing to his family. The Whitleys have been unwise in allowing these men into their home. It's a bad example for their children."

"Ben and Brian are seeing their parents love Alex and Scott unconditionally, and they know their parents aren't hypocrites who say one thing on Sunday and act another way the rest of the week."

"Kitty, you've given in to other people's desires all your life. You even went to medical school because your dad wanted you to. Why don't you use this opportunity to stop that cycle? Surely you don't go along with this. Look at what Alex and Scott are," Janet begged.

"I'm looking at *who* they are: Alex still possesses those wonderful qualities he had when he was young. As for Scott, he genuinely cared for Alex when no Christian in Hallton would even call him," Kitty replied, ignoring the other things Janet had said.

"How can you see them as normal?"

"I've read the Bible just like you. Know what? There are other things on that sin list: gossip, lying, backbiting, lust. Gossip alone would alienate everyone in church. Lying sends people to hell—ever tell Paul a partial truth? Is being gay so terrible that we're supposed to forget Alex and Scott in their time of need?" Kitty asked.

"We aren't forgetting them, but Alex needs to repent before we can fellowship with him. Kitty, there's talk of disfellowship for people who are helping the Whitleys," Janet said. "They've drawn good people like you and Harley into their deception. Please don't allow yourself to be cast out of the church."

Kitty was exasperated. "I'm not going to be intimidated by threats. I know I'm doing God's will. You need to inspect your own heart."

"My heart is fine." Janet was irritated.

"I'm talking about having a heart for people in need. There isn't any need to leave Hallton to enter a mission field. You're needed at the Whitley home. You have no idea how tired they are and how much another set of hands would help. If you'd like to see what I mean, wait around for another thirty minutes and I'll be on my way there. For the last few days Alex has required constant attention. Then of course there's the emotional toil of him slowly rotting to death.

"You should see the bloodshot eyes of everyone in that household. You can fold clothes, make a meal, rub Annie's feet or shoulders, cut their lawn, iron some clothes, clean a bathroom, or sit with Alex while Annie takes a hot bath and gets a full hour's sleep. Maybe Paul would like to help Wayne with his milking."

"Can't do it—you need to consider what this is doing to your family. Look at the hours you're spending there," Janet pleaded. "You're pregnant. What are you doing to your baby?"

"The baby is fine. I take my girls with me to help with light chores while I attend to Alex. I never heard you worry about my time when I treated your sick mother-in-law while I was pregnant with Emily."

"Is this a no?" Janet asked.

"It's a no. Tell Paul if the Whitleys go, then we go. I speak for Aunt Susan, also. We're too busy to play church politics." Kitty took the chart and left the room.

It was almost dark when Jett arrived home with his briefcase and suit coat tucked under his arm. After Clark left, Jett had visited some of his companies' stores to avoid any more people showing up unannounced. Jett busied himself in his study until the family sat down for supper. The usual spills occurred during the meal, but Donna had prepared food Will liked so there would be nothing to upset Jett. Soon after Will had finished eating, they excused him and were left to talk.

"How was your day?" Jett asked disinterestedly.

"Uneventful, except for another call from Harley. Why haven't you returned his calls?"

"I haven't had time." Jett continued to eat without looking at her.

"You've had plenty of time. So what gives? Why are you running from Alex?"

Jett looked at Donna with an angry glare. "How many times do I have to tell you? I confronted him about his homosexuality."

"Well, Harley's message is that Alex is dying."

"He's dying, so what's new? Tell me something I don't know," Jett said sarcastically. "He has AIDS and he's paying for his sin." Jett took his plate to the sink.

"I love you. I don't know why you can't be kind." Tears came into Donna's eyes. "As I've prayed, Jett, and read the Bible, uh—this has been a burden for several days now..."

Jett dropped his dish and grabbed the back of the chair. His knuckles were white. It was a nightmare. Jett felt like a trapped animal. Only God knew those were the words Alex spoke to him that fateful night.

"I've done nothing wrong! I'm tired of everyone's accusations. I've got to get out of here. Don't wait up." He was in a rage.

Jett slammed the door. As he put the key in Donna's Suburban, a hot brand of conviction penetrated every crevice of his soul. He had to run.

Jett drove with fury to the only place he felt he could get comfort. For the first time in years he felt terrified. Long ago he feared that he would go to hell for what he had done to Rita. Now he feared that Donna would leave him. Her words as he left the house kept ringing in his ears: "I'm leaving with Will for Chicago to see some friends, and I don't know when I'll be back."

It had been almost a month since the ravages of sin had begun to claw at his soul once again. Now the cold clutch of his past was backing him against the wall. What he couldn't figure out was why God would be chastising him. Why now? He had repented for what he did to Rita and their child. His sin— according to the Bible—should be removed as far as the east is from the west.

"God, I've paid for it! I've been careful not to sin anymore . . ." Jett wiped the nervous sweat that was pouring from his brow. "Don't make me see Alex!"

He slung gravel as he pulled into the driveway at Harley's home, and the automatic security lights popped on as he put his vehicle in park. It wasn't long before the kitchen door opened and Harley came outside.

"I didn't know your name was Ichabod Crane." Harley laughed as he pulled a pack of cigarettes from his shirt pocket. Taking one out of the half-filled pack, he tapped it on the box and then lit it.

"Ichabod?" Jett tried not to act nervous, knowing that Ichabod was a conservative Christian colloquialism for someone who was beyond redemption. He shivered at the comparison, feeling the heavy breath of God bearing down on his neck.

"You know: the Headless Horseman. Were you being chased by a headless horseman down Bear Lake Road?" Harley took a puff and motioned for them to walk out into the field.

"Oh no, it was nothing like that—I got distracted and almost missed my turn," Jett replied as he pushed away one of the horses that came from the field looking for a carrot in his pocket.

Harley stopped and studied him for a minute. Even in the moonlight he could see Jett's face contorting as if he was in pain.

"Are you okay?" Harley asked. "If you're worried, I'm not angry with you. I just want you to see Alex."

"That's out of the question. I can't have you forcing me to have fellowship with a non-Christian—worse, a person who has taken God's name into the pit of hell."

"I'm saying you need to do what's right." Harley tossed the cigarette onto the dirt and spoke with a hint of irritation in his voice. "In the very least you hurt Alex's feelings that night. I can figure that much out. So apologize— that's all. Apologize for being a jerk to him."

"You're pretty good at telling me what's wrong with me. Maybe you need to spend your afternoons telling Alex why he's going to hell." Jett was almost shouting. He had to talk loud enough to drown out the extremely loud beating of his heart.

"Why are you so scared of Alex?" Harley asked with a calm, kind voice.

"I'm not afraid of anyone, let alone Alex Marshall. That night he was using the scripture as a ruse to get into our room for sex."

"That's ridiculous, Jett." Harley laughed, and then he got serious again as he got into Jett's face. "Is that what you've told people? Remember me? Jett, I know what a come-on looks like—I was in prison. Find some other lie to tell. I know you well enough to recognize you're scared. You did something that night that upset Alex so much he didn't want to stay in town."

"I did *nothing*," Jett replied with an angry edge in his voice.

"Yes, you did. Want to know why I say that?" Harley looked at Jett and spoke each word distinctly. "Because after all these years, you've *never* told anyone Alex left town after seeing you."

"You're a fine one to talk about me . . ."

Harley pushed Jett with enough force that he almost fell in the clumps of dirt as he stumbled backwards. After a long hard look, Harley walked passed him toward the house.

"Where are you going? We need to settle this right now!" Jett demanded.

Harley turned. With a mix of anger and hurt he answered, "I can't believe you. And no I won't talk with you, because you just throw my sins up in my face whenever I try to get you to do the right thing for Wayne and Annie. I don't even know you anymore." Harley started walking toward the house, and then he turned again.

"Yes, I do know you, Jett—you've turned into The Coach. You've accomplished your goal. My question is what kind of man would want to be like Bill Marshall? He was cruel to the bone to his family, sought vengeance on people who tried to correct him, all the while beating his Bible and pointing a finger at others for *their* sins."

Harley walked into the house, leaving Jett alone in the darkness to think. It was late. Tomorrow would bring a new day, and once Donna left town Jett would arrange to visit a store on the West Coast. He had to leave town until Alex died.

22

WHITLEY HOME~TUESDAY NIGHT

The door to Alex's room opened and Scott walked out with a two-day-old beard, wrinkled shorts and shirt, and bloodshot eyes. The weary man sat on the sofa beside Wayne, who was watching the late-night news.

"Ready for me to take over?" Wayne sipped coffee as he watched the weather. "I've been trying to wake up for the last ten minutes."

"Kitty will be finished soon." Scott threw his head back and sighed. "I don't know, I don't know, I don't know."

"It's hard." Wayne turned off the television. "Toughest thing I ever went through: losing someone close to me. You see it coming and there's no way to stop it from happening."

"I feel like an eighteen-wheeler is bearing down on me and I'm unable to move."

Scott looked at the ceiling fan as it made a circle. The house was quiet as family members got a few short hours of sleep. All of them knew the end was close, and they were putting forth their last bit of strength. Fatigue brought high emotions—short tempers as well as tears. Wayne got up. As he stopped to pour another cup of coffee, he took a long look at Scott. There he sat, alone with his pain in a town where he was a stranger. The Whitleys had done their best to make him feel welcome, but Alex required everyone's time and strength.

How could Wayne reach out to Scott? Annie said God had given her grace to see that Alex and Scott needed a relationship with people who walked in the love of Jesus. Wayne had not been able to relate to him. Could he let down the emotional wall? Could he meet him in the middle of his grief and bring peace to his heart, like Clark said?

Once, long ago, Wayne had been in need and another man had helped him through the grief. What was the difference between helping Scott through his grief and The Coach helping him through his? Wayne sat down on the sofa again. He must talk with this man as The Coach had talked with him. No one knew anything about Scott except he was Alex's partner and he owned a newspaper. Soon Alex would be dead and Scott would be without a family.

"May I share something with you?" Wayne asked.

"Sure, but my mind is a little fuzzy," Scott smiled.

Wayne recognized it as a practiced smile, with pain buried deep inside. He fished for words to meet Scott on a more intimate level. Silently Wayne cried out to God.

"I understand what's happening to you. You see, I lost my first wife. I do understand what it feels like to lose your companion." Wayne took a swallow of coffee.

"When?" Scott asked softly.

"Twenty-five years ago. Her name was Karen. We did everything right."

"I can identify with that." Scott looked at him with interest. "What happened?"

"We had been married five years, and one day she passed out. Tests revealed that she had a congenital heart defect. We were so hopeful for a cure."

Scott nodded his head.

"On the last day of school before Christmas vacation in 1969, I came home and found her on the floor just inside the door. She was still warm, but I was too late to save her." Wayne sighed and closed his eyes.

"I appreciate your concern, but you can stop if it's too painful."

Wayne shook his head and continued.

"In that moment everything changed. Without her, nothing had meaning. I just existed. One night The Coach came over. We'd taught together and he'd known me from working here on his dad's farm when I was a kid. The Coach helped me. He'd experienced his own wife's death and could identify with my pain. He even got me to move in with him and his family. It took a while, but I began to heal. Soon the depression lifted and I had a faint desire to live. For all the bad things The Coach did to Alex, he helped a lot of people like me. The Coach told me how he got through his own wife's death. His motivation was a love for Jesus Christ."

Wayne saw he was losing Scott.

"I lived with the Marshalls for five months. I became his assistant coach, and then my eyes opened to Annie. By the time she was in college I was smitten with her, and it's still how I feel. Annie is bone of my bone. Our relationship is so different from the one I had with Karen."

"You have a great relationship." Scott smiled a genuine smile. "You have a very nice family. Your sons have treated me like—like a relative. I couldn't ask for better care, Wayne."

"Before long Alex will be gone, but we don't want to lose you, Scott. I want you to know that I'm here for you, just like The Coach was there for me." Wayne had finally been able to identify with Scott.

"You've been very kind to me. Once this nightmare is over, I'll stay in touch."

"I hope you'll do more than that, Scott. We consider you part of our family." The words came with freedom as Wayne broke the barrier that had locked up his heart since they arrived.

"I don't understand your openness." Scott was confused.

"How can I refuse to show you the same love Jesus has shown me?" Wayne's words came from the heart.

"You mean witnessing?" Scott shrank back.

"You've probably had a lifetime of that. No, Scott, I want to be your friend, if you'll let me. I have no hidden motive," Wayne replied.

Scott relaxed. "I receive stacks of hate mail every week from people who are committed Christians. Are you a conservative Christian?"

"Yes, I am. I accept the Bible as God's true word. However, with the same conviction, I want you to know it would be a sin if I didn't offer to help you carry this burden of Alex dying and the grief that will follow his death. It's too big to shoulder alone."

Wayne could hear Kitty finishing in Alex's room. It was time to get instructions for his shift. He stood to walk into the bedroom, but Scott touched his hand.

"I've never known Christians like you and Annie. Someday I want to know more about your relationship with Jesus."

"Once we've closed this chapter in our lives, we'll talk," Wayne replied, and then he walked into Alex's room.

TAYLOR HOME

Jett tossed and turned, and he awoke screaming. Donna sat up in bed.

"This has been going on for nights now. What is it?" She could see terror in his face.

"Nothing; I need to go pray."

He jumped from the bed, put on his robe, and went into his office across the hall. Donna prayed as she watched him go. The last few years she had witnessed Jett's slow regression from the man with the positive influence to someone driven by perfectionism and arrogance over his celebrated spiritual commitment. His sermons were laced with legalism. So much of his communication with their son was dotted with subtle talk of 'being a man.' It was much like how she remembered The Coach.

The Coach had been a thorn in her flesh from the day she married Jett. While he pretended to "love and adore Jett's little woman," she knew it was just a ploy to keep Jett happy. Whenever he could, The Coach would bring up Rita. To him Rita was the perfect girl: acquiescent to everything Jett said or wanted, beautiful beyond belief, and quiet.

Donna, on the other hand, certainly spoke her mind whenever it was necessary. Once she had heard The Coach tell his grandson Brian that he was a 'sissy like his uncle'—meaning Alex. Donna waited until they were alone and let The Coach clearly know that talk like that was unacceptable. He didn't like what she said, but The Coach never told Jett either.

The Coach was very specific about what made a man. She had seen Harley joke about his 'manhood' by flexing muscles; Jett could never do anything like that. At first she thought maybe Jett and Alex had had an intimate, spur-of-the-moment incident happen between them. However, Jett's answer that Sunday had been so honest, she knew there was something else he was running from.

Tomorrow morning Donna was planning to take Will to see some friends in Chicago. She needed a break. Her return date was still up in the air. While she wanted to be there for Annie and Wayne at Alex's funeral, her anger at Jett would boil to a sinful level if she was around to see him continue in this vendetta. Before she left tomorrow Donna would give Kitty a call to explain.

"Don't let Jett rest until your work is complete, Father." She rolled over and went back to sleep.

❧ ❧ ❧

In solemn seclusion, Jett fell to his knees.

"Lord, I'm worried about Donna's trip. Please, keep them from harm. Put your angels around them."

Concern about the trip was not what was making his sleep restless and his days full of anxiety. Jett turned his prayers to Harley and Kitty, then to Susan Spencer, and finally to Clark Perkins. Yet the weight of his burden would not end. He went through name after name until he began praying for Annie and Wayne.

"Give them wisdom, Lord, in how to handle Alex. Lord, save Alex—please, God."

A fiery sensation ravaged him from his chest to his head. It was the pain of his nightmares. He got to his feet and stumbled into his desk chair weeping with fear and trepidation.

"Please, God, just let him die. He's going to die soon."

His mind rushed with thoughts about Alex with his lover Scott. Seeing Alex would be—he did not know what. They were never close, so his demise would not be a loss. The death of The Coach almost killed him because he felt as if he had lost his father. Alex deserved to suffer for the way he treated The Coach. This illness was a curse on Alex for the way he lived his life.

Jett reflected on the sermons he had preached about AIDS. He had warned that AIDS was God's judgment on the gay community. Even with Brian present, Jett had talked about former members of the church who had run from God to homosexuality. Alex had been unrepentant all these years. Annie and Wayne were wrong in bringing him back to Hallton with his lover.

What were they thinking? How could they justify having these two men in their home? Maybe I ought to satisfy everyone and go see Alex, try to get him to repent.

Jett opened his calendar.

"See, God. I told you I wasn't free," Jett said as he looked down the pages. However, time was short, and he knew God would not let him rest until he saw Alex.

"God, I can't talk with him." Jett gasped for air. "It goes against all I stand for. Lord, you know I've sinned, but not like Alex. He's refused to come out of his lifestyle, and I've sinned no more. How can I be a Christian if I don't hold a tough line on those who take your name into the very pit of hell?"

After hours of crying, Jett sat without moving, thinking about his sin. He knew it was too late to rectify the wrongs he had committed against Rita. It wasn't too late with Alex, but how could he take this disease-ravaged man into his arms like Jesus? Half-man, really, because Alex's passion raged for another man. Could Jett accept Alex even though Alex hadn't repented? Jett was staring out the window when he heard Donna. She stopped in the doorway as the clock struck five.

"I heard you." Donna was concerned because Jett rarely shed a tear.

"How can I do it?" Jett asked soberly.

"Do what, honey?" she said as she sat in the chair across from him.

"How can I love Alex unconditionally?"

Donna thought about it. "Jett, how can you not love him—after what Jesus has done for us?" Then she added, "Alex has been in a type of prison all these years: isolated from his family and friends. You hold the key to open that prison door."

"Why do you say that?"

"You know in your heart that Jesus would do exactly what Annie and Wayne are doing, Jett. But from the time Annie and Wayne came to you, you've done nothing but spread dissension. Why?"

"Alex's lover isn't a girl. He's a guy just like Alex, and they kiss. They have sex. All of this is an abomination to God," Jett argued, his voice becoming louder with each word.

"Alex will die soon. Can he be reached by finger-pointing? If Alex can't see Jesus operating in our lives, then we need to assess what we're doing wrong and change."

"But Alex knows he's gone against the Word of God, and he's never repented." Jett sat straight in his chair.

"I'm not going to debate, Jett. You don't realize that the finger of judgment you point at Alex has actually come back and punched holes in your heart. Your soul has been affected by this." Donna stopped and steadied herself for a potential argument because of the question she was about to ask.

"I'll ask you one more time: What happened that night in Green Bay that has made you so afraid of Alex?" Donna asked. "Until you can truthfully answer this question your heart will continue to have darkness."

Jett's confidence went out the window. Donna was speaking words that God would say to him. He bit his lower lip.

Donna continued, "Alex needs to know that God has loved him all these years. Jett, you've got to make it right ..."

Jett broke down into sobs. Donna got up and walked to him.

"I've never seen you like this," Donna whispered as she hugged him.

"Shut the door. We need to talk."

ℯ ℯ ℯ

Donna studied the carpet beneath her bare feet. Her eyes were now dry. The morning rays came in softly through the stained-glass window of Jett's study. She could see the image of David and Goliath in mosaics from the corner of her eye. Her feet interested her. So many times she had seen those feet buried in the foreign soil when she was a missionary in Kenya. Now the same feet were buried in plush carpet. She longed for the simplicity of those bygone days. Jett sat trembling before her, but he couldn't look in her eyes.

"Aren't you going to say anything?" he asked, in a hoarse whisper.

Donna stood up, paced around the room, and then stopped at a framed magazine cover.

"You were featured in *Sports Illustrated*." She turned to him and quoted: "Jett Taylor is the man who has it all. He's claimed all the world's prizes from football and now retires to serve God and raise a family."

From there Donna walked over to his desk and picked up his Super Bowl ring. "Along the way you got this." She put it on her finger and gave Jett an icy stare. "When you got this and wore it so proudly, did you ever once think about all the lives you ruined?"

Jett looked down at his lap. "No."

Donna threw the ring at him, hitting his shoulder. The direct hit did not compare to the pain of her words. Brushing back the hair from her face, Donna stuck her index finger into his chest.

"That's scary, Jett. You're responsible for two people dying and now a third. You're guilty of a lot of things, but the worst is spiritual pride. You must decide who you're going to serve."

As she opened the door, fear enveloped Jett like a glove. "What are you going to do? Please don't leave me—please," he begged.

"Don't worry about me. If I were you, I'd worry more about whether Alex Marshall will die before you have a chance to ask his forgiveness."

Donna walked out of the room, leaving Jett in stone silence. She had spoken the truth. What could he do? Jett moved his hand toward the phone. What would he say? Worse yet, what if Wayne wouldn't let him in the house? For years Jett had used Alex as a scapegoat. As he dialed the numbers, Jett felt he would become violently ill.

"Wayne?"

"Yes. Who is this, please?" Wayne replied with a sleepy voice.

"It's Jett. Wayne, I need to see Alex." His voice trembled.

"That isn't possible. I can't have you causing trouble. He's too sick."

"Please. Wayne, please. I must talk to him before he dies. I have to make my peace . . ." Jett's voice broke.

The silence tore at Jett's insides. He could hear Wayne talk with Annie, and then Wayne's voice was back on the line.

"You can come at ten. If Alex is unable to see you, you'll have to leave. See you then." Wayne hung up.

Jett put down the receiver and held his head in his hands. "Please, God, let him live until I see him."

Jett immediately picked up the phone again and pushed the speed dial. After three rings Harley answered.

"I'm going to see Alex today. Do you have time to talk?" Jett asked, and then he interrupted what Harley was about to say.

"I need to tell you what happened that night Alex came to see me in Green Bay. I used him as an excuse to ignore my own sins," Jett said. "First, I need to ask your forgiveness for last night, as well as throwing your past in your face a couple of Sundays ago . . ."

After his apology, Jett began his story.

23

WHITLEY HOME~WEDNESDAY, JUNE 29

THE CLOCK STRUCK TEN and there was a knock at the front door. Annie and Wayne greeted Jett. His eyes were puffy and his face was crimson. Wayne spoke to him in the living room.

"Brian is working in the barn, and we've sent Ben with Scott on an errand. Alex has been very coherent this morning; better than he's been for two days. If you upset him in any way, you will never be welcome in our home again. Is that understood?"

"I won't cause a problem." Jett kept his head down. "I need to talk with your family once I finish with Alex."

"I'll be in the kitchen with Annie." Wayne's voice was less harsh this time.

"He's in there." Annie walked Jett to the bedroom door.

"Thanks." Jett walked through the white enameled door.

On the hospital bed lay the yellow, frail body. Right now Jett deserved to lose everything because of what he had done to Rita, their baby, and Alex. There would be no more running, no more hurting and using people like he had used Harley. Jett's soul was as sick as Alex's body, and it was time to make it right.

Hearing Jett's voice made Alex's head throb. Without Calvin's urging, this meeting would never have taken place. Jett pulled the cane chair close to Alex's bedside, but he stared at the floor.

"I know I look gross." Alex spoke slowly, but with a new inner strength. "This disease is like wrestling a tiger that won't let me go."

"Alex," Jett choked back the tears, "I'm sorry—I'm sorry you're sick."

"Thanks." Alex relaxed a little. "I'm glad you're here, because I wanted to tell you I have no hard feelings."

"I need a favor." Jett wiped the tears from his eyes.

"I'm limited in what I can do." Alex managed a weak smile. "But if I can . . ."

The breeze blew through the window. The stench of sickness was thick. Jett still would not look at Alex or the symbols of his impending death: the IV, the bags for body fluid, and the bedpans. In the corner was a sofa with pillows and a light blanket where someone had spent the night. Death was close.

"Tell me what you came to tell me that night," Jett appealed.

"What night?"

"The night I said those horrible things to you and drove you away; the night you had scripture for me. Tell me what God wanted me to know." Jett was humble. He bit his lower lip and his hands shook. He knew that his soul would never rest until Alex delivered the message.

"Jett, that was a long time ago, and you were right all along. I didn't belong in Hallton." Alex was trying to make peace with Jett, but, as well, he truly didn't want to discuss that evening.

"I need to know—please, Alex." Tears fell from Jett's eyes.

Alex's heart pounded with fear as it had that night. It was as if he was back in that hotel room.

"Alex, I was afraid of what you were going to say. I recognized you as a messenger from God. I didn't want the message, so I vilified you. All these years you've paid for my sin. I need to know what you were coming to tell me." Jett paused. "I'm *so sorry* for the way I acted toward you."

Jett's honesty gave Alex the courage to speak.

"As I studied my Bible, there was one passage that stuck out. Day after day I opened my Bible to the same place. Each time I read the verse I thought about you. I prayed for you, but this heavy oppression would come and I felt like something bad was happening to you. I had never experienced anything like that before. It continued for several weeks."

"Which verse?"

"It was very odd, because the verse was positive and not foreboding. I thought maybe God wanted you to remember the plan he had for your life. Jett, I honestly had no idea. The verse was from Jeremiah 1, the one about God knowing us before he formed us in the womb . . ."

Jett burst forth with a cry that came from deep within his soul, and he sobbed uncontrollably. Wayne was at the door in an instant, but he closed it when he saw that Alex was okay. After a long time Jett regained his composure. His chin quivered with each word he spoke.

"I was riding high with football and everyone wanted me to speak for their youth gatherings, and then there was Rita," Jett sighed.

"She was beautiful and was so in love with you. Whatever became of her?"

"I'm the reason she's dead. What you had to tell me would have stopped it." Jett stopped and tried to gather the words to continue. "Rita was my first love and I wanted to spend the rest of my life with her. I had every intention of cherishing her as God wanted me to, but I didn't."

"I remember you brought her to meet The Coach at Christmas," Alex said. "It was evident that you loved her."

"We became intimate. At first I had a lot of guilt, but I justified it since we were going to get married. I thought I could handle every temptation without answering to anyone. When I failed I couldn't tell anyone."

"Don't be too hard on yourself, Jett; you learned that from The Coach. He felt real men were to handle all their problems without help," Alex offered.

"Maybe so, but I can't blame him for everything. I'd have married Rita at any time, but her father wanted her to complete grad school first. She had two more semesters when I got her pregnant." Jett looked at Alex. "I *really* loved her, and I wanted lots of babies with her, but not at that time. I panicked. The only thing I knew to do was arrange for an abortion."

"You? I'm shocked. You always preached against it."

"Desperation will drive a man to do many things he never thought he'd do. Rita wanted to have the baby, but I wore her down. I promised her that we'd marry the minute she finished school."

"She bought it?"

"I got materials from organizations that said it was only fetal tissue and not a life. Ultrasound wasn't as sophisticated then, so she accepted everything I said. I did whatever it took to hush up the matter. No one knew, not even Harley. If people found out, it'd have ruined my ministry—how ridiculous that sounds now." Jett shook his head. "I could have handled the bad press, but not your father's rejection. He'd have written me off. The Coach could never forgive a person for his weakness."

Alex smiled tenderly. "He was very strict, but you were everything to him. The Coach would have been furious, but eventually he'd have forgiven you. I'm sure you know that."

"I never wanted to find out. I never missed any goal your dad set for me. When I was young, I had this void." Jett placed his hand over his heart. "I had such a profound need for a father. The loss of that relationship would have been more than I could bear. I spent all my life competing with you for his affection. I realized you were God's messenger that night in Green Bay. I wanted to make sure you'd never tell anyone, especially The Coach . . . that's why I said all those horrible things." Jett buried his face on the bed and began to cry again. The words "I'm so sorry" came with great effort.

"Don't be sorry, Jett," Alex said. "I needed to get away from here. The Coach made my life hell. Did the abortion have something to do with Rita's death?"

Jett gazed out the window as a flood welled again in his eyes. "Rita had the abortion the day after you came to my room. After the game I took her to a clinic. I thought I had every base covered, but she fell into a depression so deep she wasn't able to function. The semester had barely started, but within weeks she quit school. I moved from New York to Pittsburgh to be near her. She wasn't up to getting married after that. Then about the time the baby would have been born, when I was away at spring training camp, Rita . . . killed herself."

"I'm so sorry." Tears came to Alex's eyes.

"I was devastated. No one had any idea why Rita was depressed, let alone the timing of her suicide. By then I was a master of protecting myself, so I never let on. God brought you home, and I was forced to stop running and face my sin."

"Why did you tell me? You could have kept it a secret forever," Alex said.

"God hasn't let me rest since Annie and Wayne told us about your illness. Alex, I'm responsible for you leaving. Not only that, in fear that my sin would be uncovered. I always made you out to be the villain in my head. I sinned against you that night in the same way I sinned against Rita and our child."

With sincere and spontaneous humility Jett dropped to his knees and pressed his face against Alex's yellowed hand. "Please forgive me for those horrible things I said that night and for all the years I made your life hell. Forgive me for taking your father from you."

Alex lifted Jett's chin with the tips of his shaking fingers. "Please, get up. I forgive you for everything."

"I'd like to make a public apology at church with you there. I've been very vocal against you through the years." Jett stood and wiped his tears with both hands.

"I can't walk. My time is very short, so don't do anything on my behalf. Just knowing what you've told me is enough." Alex pointed to the apparatus by the bed. "Give me oxygen, and then I have a confession to make to you."

Jett helped get the oxygen, and then he took a cloth and wiped Alex's face.

"I can't believe that you have anything to confess to me."

"I've kept a secret from you. I'll tell you as much as I know, and then I need for you to talk with Harley's mother. Annie also needs to know, but telling her will be up to you. Promise me that you'll do this for me."

"Yes, but what is it? Why Ella Hamilton?"

"Do you remember the day Harley's dad was called because you stole something from a grocery store?"

"How did you know? I thought it was a secret," Jett sputtered with a knee-jerk reaction.

"Don't worry. Tom never told anyone but The Coach." Alex reached toward Jett and emphasized. "*No one knew*. Honest. My window was up and I happened to overhear a conversation in my front yard. You're the first person I've ever told."

"Why was Tom talking with The Coach about me? I had no idea he knew," Jett said. "He never let on."

"Maybe he felt guilty. Now listen carefully, Jett, to what I have to say: that night Tom asked why The Coach hadn't done anything for you and your mom. Tom said that you had tried to steal because you were so poor," Alex said.

"Why would Tom ask The Coach that question, of all people? That incident was at least a few months before I got involved in one of The Coach's peewee football camps. It's not like we had a relationship at the time."

"Stay with me on this, Jett, because it's very important that you hear what I have to say. The Coach got angry. Tom said, 'I told you three years ago that you needed to take care of your family. When are you going to accept responsibility for what you did?' Then The Coach responded with something about your mom being a slut." Alex stopped to get some oxygen.

"The Coach called my mom a slut?" Jett had not grasped everything Alex just said.

Alex was tired, but he knew he must continue. He spoke slowly. Jett had to hear how the conversation had unfolded years ago.

"Tom said, 'If you don't assume some responsibility for your son, I'll do it through the courts.' The Coach said, 'You can't prove anything.' Then Tom threw him against a tree and said, 'You were her teacher, and in legal terms it's called rape. It's time for you to own up to your sin.'"

"You're not saying The Coach was my father?" Jett staggered at this revelation.

"Yes, The Coach was your father, but that's all I know. You must find out the rest from Ella." Alex breathed some more oxygen. "Please, and then tell Annie everything. She's much too tired to hear this now."

"Why didn't he tell me? I begged him to let me be his son, because I needed a father so much. I thought he loved me." Jett looked at Alex with compassion, but inside his anger toward The Coach started growing.

Jett became silent, but it was evident that his mind was working on all Alex had said.

"And he called my mother a slut? She was barely fifteen when *he* got her pregnant. How old was he?" Hot tears began to roll down his face.

"At least ten years older than your mom. Jett, The Coach was the slut."

Jett was gentle as he spoke. "You're my brother?"

Jett stood and looked at Alex. No longer was Alex a gay man with a terrible disease, but his brother. If Jett hadn't come to confess, then he would never have known how deeply they were connected.

Alex grasped Jett, and the shackles fell off his heart. For the first time in decades he was free. The anger of a lifetime evaporated. His anger toward God was gone. Alex began to cry. He felt restored to his family, his town, and the faith of his youth.

Jett helped him get settled in bed, gave him some water, and wiped his face with a cool cloth.

"I've betrayed your family—my family—and now I need to tell Annie and Wayne about that night in Green Bay," Jett spoke with compassion. "I want to get to know you before you die."

"I'd like to get to know you, too," Alex said.

24

FRIDAY, JULY 1

Scott spent the better part of the morning composing a tribute to Alex and his family, which would be the editorial in next week's *Pride Position*. He read it once more before faxing it to Lesley. In it, he praised the Whitley family for showing the love of Christ. Scott knew there were few words adequate to describe this week, especially the day Jett came to see Alex.

It had been noon on Wednesday when Scott and Ben returned from Kitty's office, arms full of medical supplies. When Scott saw Jett emerging from Alex's room with a puffy face streaked with tears, for a moment he thought Alex had died.

One by one the Whitley family gathered in the kitchen and sat at the table. Harley came into the room as Jett was gathering courage. The words were slow in coming. Harley pulled a chair behind Jett and rubbed his back. Scott was privy to Jett's private moment—like a man telling his unsuspecting wife he's been unfaithful.

Little by little, Jett told them about being intimate with Rita, her pregnancy, why he suggested an abortion, and Rita's suicide. Annie reached out to comfort him just as he began to tell of the night in Green Bay, but she stopped mid-air with a look of horror on her face when it became clear what he was saying.

Annie said, "You mean all those years we came to you for prayer because we were so confused about what happened to Alex, and you were the reason he left?" As she grasped Jett's treachery, she recoiled as if a poisonous snake was ready to bite her.

Brian glared at him with tears already splashing down his face. "How could you?'"

Wayne got up from his chair and walked outside.

Annie turned to Harley, and betrayal mixed with anger was felt in each word. "Did you know?"

"I was there that night for a minute, but I left. I didn't know what happened until early this morning. I'm sorry, Annie . . . Wayne . . ." Harley's voice trailed off.

Jett hung his head and tears dropped onto the linoleum floor. No one got near him except Harley. He was like someone with a plague. Brian went to be with Alex. Silent seconds became silent minutes.

Wayne came into the room and walked over to Jett. As Wayne raised his arms, Jett shrank back. Any other man would have struck Jett. Instead, Wayne slipped his arms down over Jett in a hug. He knelt down so he could have eye contact with Jett who was too ashamed to lift his head.

"I'm so sorry," Jett said over and over again to Wayne.

Wayne spoke. "A wise man once told me a real man brings peace to another man's heart. Jett, you haven't had peace for a long time. Because Jesus forgave me, I can forgive you."

Annie joined Wayne and pulled Harley into the group. Ben left the room and returned with Brian. He got on his knees alongside his father. Scott stared at them. Scott was furious for the hurt Jett had caused Alex. The Whitleys, though, were a portrait of the unselfish love that forgives a sin of this magnitude. It was a portrait of Christ loving his children—a picture of grace.

For two days the scene haunted Scott.

If they could forgive Jett, can I forgive my father? Can Dad forgive me? Can Jesus ever be that genuine for me?

Scott faxed his editorial to *The Pride Position*. As he waited for confirmation it had gone through, he bowed his head.

"Jesus, I'm willing to trust you. I want you to be real and not a crutch. I want to know you like Annie and Wayne know you."

AUSTIN MEMORIAL PARK

"Well, sugar, I'm packed and will be gone by this time the day after tomorrow." Samuel sounded content for the first time in months. He unrolled his sandwich as the breeze carried away the napkin that had held it.

"I know I haven't been by here much lately, but I've been helping people. Another woman whose sister is the victim of abuse came by the house to see if I could find her a safe place. It really feels good. Esther told me that Brent Cooley finally decided to go to counseling. She didn't know who Brent was going to see, but at least he's willing."

Samuel was quiet as he took a bite and chewed.

Swallowing, he said, "Big news for you—I've arranged a layover in Atlanta. I'm going to try to get in touch with Scott and see if he'll talk to me. I don't blame him if he doesn't, but at least I've tried." Samuel smiled. "I'm going to try everything, Nat, to let him know I love him."

PART FOUR

❧ The Pardon ☙

A prison cell, in which one waits, hopes, and is completely dependent on the fact that the door of freedom has to be opened from the outside, is not a bad picture of Advent.

Dietrich Bonhoeffer

25

HALLTON~SUNDAY MORNING, JULY 3

Wayne awoke on Sunday morning with a sense of peace in his soul that went
beyond his understanding. As he walked down the stairs he smelled bleach and
heard the washing machine churning. He grabbed a cup of coffee from the
bottomless pot that had been brewing since Annie had returned to Hallton.

At the table Annie sat talking with Susan, who was preparing breakfast.
Calvin's mother, Mary, was folding the latest set of clean linens. Seeing
Annie's and Mary's rumpled hair and bloodshot eyes, Wayne knew they had
not slept. They turned to acknowledge him as he poured the coffee.

"Scott's on the front porch, dear, if you'd like to talk with him," Annie
said slowly, her battery running low. "Harley will be here in twenty minutes
to help set up for the worship service. I'm letting the boys sleep as long as
they can."

"Sweetheart, you need rest." Wayne gave her a hug. "So do you, Mary."

Mary smiled as she folded sheets. She was as faithful to the Whitleys as
she was to her own husband and son. There would never be any way Wayne
could repay the Johnson family.

"Our borrowed time is about to run out," Annie said. "There'll be plenty of time for sleep in the days ahead, but meanwhile I'm going to rest my feet and back until it's time for the service."

Wayne noticed the dark circles under Annie's eyes. He had promised Alex he could die at home, but Wayne would need to put him in the hospital if his condition continued much longer. As he passed Alex's room, he saw Jett asleep with his head on the bed. What a radical change had occurred in the past four days! Each day Jett spent hours holding Alex's hand, and when Alex was able, they talked about their lives. Jett had even gone on a few walks with Scott. Jett's contrition was helping everyone to forgive his deception.

Jett's confession was like a hot knife piercing Wayne's soul. For years Jett had prayed with them about Alex's reprobate condition. Not once during their agony had Jett offered the truth. When he admitted his betrayal, Wayne could have killed him with his bare hands, but with Annie's help he was able to forgive Jett.

Jett had asked to have the morning church service in the yard under Alex's window. Clark Perkins gave his blessing. The chairman of the elders, Amos Connor, came over to get everything prepared. Even in his advancing years, Amos was excited about what the Lord was doing. Calvin had canceled the services at his own church and encouraged his congregation to come to the Whitleys, where he felt the Lord would have an important message for them on this day. There were others, however, who were not so supportive of their efforts to bring God to Alex.

Wayne opened the squeaky wooden screen door and walked out onto the porch with his mug. "In the winter we have a storm door, but for the summer we put this old one on the hinges. It's been a part of this house since it was built."

Scott sat looking at the fields. "It's a nice sound."

"I need to talk with you about today." Wayne sat in the rocking chair next to Scott. "It's a miracle Alex is still with us, but our time has about run out."

"I agree. His fever is erratic and he was delirious through most of the night."

"Today, I'm telling you what to do." Wayne spoke in a tone of finality.

"I'm listening." Scott was now full of trust for the Whitleys.

"You eat a good breakfast. Food will replenish the energy you need, and then stay with Alex. I don't want you to miss any time with him. I can't second-guess the Lord, but I believe today is Alex's day to go Home."

The screen door opened and Jett walked out, smoothing back his hair and putting on his glasses. "God answered my prayers. Alex is still with us."

"I pray he lasts through the morning," Wayne said.

"I'm going home to shower, change, and then be back by nine. Is that all right with you?"

"Take your time. I'll have plenty of help putting the chairs up in the yard. Is Donna back?" Wayne asked, rocking and sipping his coffee.

"She got back last night. Will is still with friends. Donna said she'd be here early to help Annie," Jett said.

"We appreciate everyone's help. Just take it easy. You haven't had much sleep, so be alert when you drive," Wayne replied.

Jett got into his car and was off in a trail of dust. Wayne and Scott went into the house to get breakfast. Susan met them at the door with a broom. She was taking a moment to sweep when a car pulled into the driveway. The driver got out and marched up the walk.

"Here comes trouble."

Paul Linder looked different—so rigid, showing none of his down-home qualities. He kept a determined pace as he walked up the stairs to the porch. Susan blocked the entrance to the house.

"Paul, we're really busy today. If you need something, let me handle it."

"Aunt Susan, I need to talk with Wayne." Paul pushed past her and through the front door.

From the living room, Wayne escorted Scott to the door of Alex's room. Paul stared into the bedroom with disdain when he saw Scott pull a chair to the edge of Alex's bed. Wayne shut the door to give Scott and Alex privacy.

"I'd like to speak with you outside," Paul demanded.

Paul waited on the porch until Wayne joined him. When Susan saw Paul would not speak with her, she went inside.

"What are you doing with these people here?" Paul said loudly when Wayne emerged from the house.

"My brother-in-law is dying," Wayne said.

"I've come to you as a brother in the Lord. It's time you stop allowing this immoral behavior in your home. You're a deacon. Unless you cease coddling sin, you'll be discharged from that office."

"Let's go out to the yard. I don't want my guests to hear." Wayne gave him a slight nudge with his left hand while pointing with his right, leading the way to the middle of the yard. Scott had come from the bedroom out to the porch, where Susan and Annie joined him.

"There's nothing immoral going on in my house," Wayne said firmly.

"That's a lie, Wayne Whitley. You just closed the door on Alex and his boyfriend." Paul poked Wayne's chest with his index finger.

"Get your mind out of the gutter. My brother-in-law is dying. He barely made it through the night. I've asked Scott to spend as much time as he can with him today."

"Are you having church services at your home today?" Paul asked.

"We're setting up in a few minutes, but I didn't have to tell you that. You need to get on with your business so I can get on with mine."

"The elders and deacons who haven't followed your deadly game of compromise are meeting to determine the future course of our church. Jett resigned on Wednesday. Did you know that?"

"Apparently Jett didn't feel it was important to tell us in light of what we're experiencing," Wayne replied.

"Your family is very close to being disfellowshipped from the church. At first, we thought it was a gesture of good faith for Annie to see her brother. Even bringing him back was kind, but when you allowed his boyfriend to come into our community, it was the last straw."

"We're proud to have Scott in our home. After Alex dies we'll continue to have a relationship with him. He's part of our family," Wayne said.

"He's part of your family? Wake up before you send your family to hell. You have two gay men in your home and you act like it's nothing. You've gone against the Bible. When two men burn . . ."

"Paul, I've walked with the Lord for half my life, and I'm doing his will. You and I have been friends all our lives. If you disagree, then that's your choice. I'm not interested in any further discussion. You need to leave so I can get back to my work." Wayne walked over to open Paul's car door.

"We'll meet today and remove you as deacon," Paul warned. "We must get our church back into line with correct thinking. Wayne, we're giving you another chance to come around—repent."

"My relationship with the Lord isn't based on a title in the church or on your approval. You do what you need to and I'll do what I need to."

"Wayne, it's dangerous to your spiritual well-being to continue thinking like you do."

Wayne studied his friend. He wished Paul could see beyond such a strict interpretation of the Bible.

"Paul, one day a problem blew headlong into my family that couldn't be solved through any standard religious formula. It hasn't been easy to step out of our comfort zone. Paul, this is the bottom line: there's no other time to be with Alex. Once he passes away then we need to be there to help Scott shoulder his loss. If you can't handle that, then I'm sorry. For my family nothing else matters except loving these two men."

Wayne turned and walked toward the house. For the first time he saw his audience on the porch. Paul got into his car, slammed the door, and threw gravel with his tires as he left the Whitley home. He was out of sight when Scott approached Wayne. Together they watched the dust settle.

"Thanks. I've never had anyone support me like that. I'm sorry I brought these problems into your home."

Wayne hugged him. "You aren't a problem. I only wish I had those seven years back to show you and Alex how much I love you both."

Scott could say nothing. His heart was too overwhelmed for words.

❧ ❧ ❧

The head of the bed was pushed close to the window so Alex could hear the service. His fever had come down, and occasionally he was able to converse. Scott sat in a chair and Annie sat at the foot of the bed.

Jett, Harley, and Donna greeted people as Wayne talked with a couple on the side of the lawn. About thirty adults and half as many youth and children arrived and were milling about in the yard until Wayne signaled the start of the service. They began by singing a few traditional hymns. Up front, Jett had the appearance of a soldier going to battle. Donna's head was erect, and she stood by his side holding his hand.

Alex closed his eyes and listened as Jett began his sermon on the Prodigal Son.

Scott's head filled with thoughts of his father. *Would Dad weep if I returned home?*

Jett shifted the sermon to the point of view of the selfish brother who stayed at home as he began his own story. Donna wiped her tears. Even the birds were silent as Jett unraveled his story about the night in Green Bay.

Alex said in a weak voice, "Annie, I forgot to answer you."

She turned from the window and smiled at him. "Sweetheart, I didn't say anything."

"Yes, you did, in Atlanta. I never told you that I forgive you." Alex smiled with all the strength he could muster.

Annie hugged him. "I love you so much, and I'm going to miss you."

"I'll see you on the other side," he said with great effort. He slowly patted her arm and closed his eyes. His breathing was steady but had become shallow in the last few hours.

Outside, Jett was closing the service when Truman Johnson, Calvin's father, stood up.

"I'd like to ask forgiveness from the white people. For many years I've had a grudge in my heart because I was born black. This has kept me from being who God intended."

Steadying himself on his cane, Amos Connor walked over to Truman. "In the '60s, I was vocal against having black people come to our church. Forgive me, Truman. I've contributed to your feeling of isolation."

The two men hugged. A heavyset man in the audience stood up.

"I never told anyone, but I've been angry at Brother Clark since he changed our services. A small thing, but when I came to church my mind focused on what he had changed, not how God was working."

Clark Perkins ran to embrace the man. Then a nice-looking man stood. "I've had a problem with lust. It's me, not my wife." He began to cry. Harley was quickly by this man's side.

One at a time people came forward to confess their sins. Scott had never seen anything like it. People were baring their souls and asking forgiveness for all kinds of sins. Most were small, but some were things that people would never tell their closest friends. It was after noon when Scott looked at his watch. He got up and started to walk out of the room.

"Is everything okay?" Annie inquired.

"I just need to make a call." Scott motioned toward the room where his office was located.

Scott walked into his small room and closed the door. Before he began to dial, he closed his eyes. Never had his heart held such conviction. But today was different—he knew he had to make a decision about a relationship with Jesus Christ.

"Jesus, forgive me of my sins. I don't understand how some things could be different, but I want to serve you. Please come into my heart. I want you to be as real to me as you are to these people."

He then picked up the receiver and dialed the phone.

26

FIRST CHURCH, AUSTIN

IN TWO MORE RINGS the phone would switch over to voice mail. Esther was in the hall greeting people, but she wondered if it could be Samuel. He was due to depart from Atlanta soon. She had made the flight changes and all morning had kept an ear out for the phone to hear the news—hoping it would be good. Another ring and Esther slipped from the crowd, grabbing the receiver just before the switch was made.

"Pastor's office, this is Esther McClanahan." She puffed from the sprint in her high heels.

"Esther? Hi, this is Scott. May I speak with my dad?"

From that moment everything was in slow motion for Esther—like being in a car wreck. She did not know if she could speak or would just pass out.

"Scott?" She grabbed a pencil and piece of paper. "Where are you?"

"I'm in Wisconsin. Is Dad there?" Scott was pleased that she was obviously delighted to hear from him.

"He's in Atlanta! He planned to make contact with you today. This afternoon he's leaving the country. I have a letter in my desk explaining all of this to you."

"Is Mom with him?" Scott asked.

Esther hesitated and cleared her throat. "Scott, your mother died a few months ago. Since that time your father has changed a great deal."

"Mom's dead?" Scott's eyes flooded with tears. He could barely embrace what had just been said, because of the powerful emotions that were raging in his soul. Already reeling from the service and Alex's impending death, Scott went numb.

"I'm very sorry, Scott. May I get your number? I'll try to reach your father before he leaves Atlanta. Tell me again, where are you?"

"Hallton, Wisconsin—outside of Green Bay. I'm staying with Wayne and Annie Whitley. The number is 414-555-8901. If you reach him, will you please give him a message?"

"Anything you want." Esther was writing as fast as she could.

"Tell him that I'm sorry and ask him if he'll forgive me."

Esther's throat swelled as she responded. "I'll be sure to tell him. Is it okay if he calls you?" She grabbed a tissue from the top of the desk for her eyes.

Scott felt his heart warm at the thought of speaking to his dad again.

"Sure. I'd like that. I need to go now, but thanks again."

Esther's hands were shaking as she put down the receiver. The press of the crowd was a nuisance.

Addressing them, Esther said, "Everyone, I need to make an emergency phone call. I'll take care of your questions after I've settled this matter. Please leave this office."

"That's highly unprofessional of you, Esther." Gerald walked over to where she stood in the doorframe.

"I'll talk with you after I make my calls." With that she closed the door, aware that it was always open on Sunday.

She steadied her hand to dial the airline. She had fifteen minutes to catch Samuel before his plane took off from Atlanta. He must feel utterly defeated by not finding Scott at home, Esther thought. The phone to the airline rang and rang, and then a voice came on the line.

"This is Esther McClanahan trying to reach a passenger, Dr. Samuel Phillips. He's set to depart for Lima, Peru, on American flight 1791. This is an emergency, and I must make contact with the plane before it takes off."

"If you'll hold the line, I'll connect you to the terminal. What's your message?"

"Tell Dr. Phillips he must not go to Peru and to call me immediately. Please, can you help me?" Esther begged.

"I've got the terminal now. Please hold."

Esther could hear voices in the background as she prayed. Five minutes passed before the representative came back with her message.

"Dr. Phillips is on the line. You can speak with him now. Go ahead."

"Samuel? Samuel, Scott called," Esther cried into the receiver.

"What?"

"Scott called to ask you . . ." Esther stopped as her voice broke. It seemed like an eternity before she could continue with the message. "He said he was sorry, and would you forgive him?"

From the other end of the line came the sobs of a father whose prayers had been answered.

27

HALTON ⁓ SUNDAY EVENING

THE SOUND OF THE bouncing ball came through the back screen door. Shooting hoops was Scott's way of dealing with Alex's death. Annie and Wayne watched as the undertaker from Krantz and Dauer took Alex's body from their house, Annie's head resting on Wayne's chest while he held her tight. She was too tired to cry and too thankful to be sad. God had redeemed Alex through their efforts.

The house was quiet. Susan busied herself in the kitchen. Kitty drank another glass of water as she completed her paperwork. Harley took Ben home with him.

Jett walked outside to join Scott as Alex's body was taken out of the house. Trading the ball back and forth, each was lost in his own thoughts. Finally Jett spoke.

"How may I help?"

"You've done all you can. I'm grateful that you came forward. When he died he was like a new man," Scott replied. "He was my best friend. I loved him so much."

Scott ached to hold his partner one more time. He could not comprehend how he would go on. He was thankful to have these people who called him their friend.

"Your honesty has had a big impact on me," Scott said as he faced Jett. "I've made a commitment to Jesus. I don't know what that means yet, but I want to see what he has for me. I'm not sure what I'll do after we bury Alex. Annie and Wayne have asked me to stay, but I need to get back to our—uh, Atlanta."

They played until the sun started to set. When they came back to the house, they found Wayne, Annie, and Brian seated around the kitchen table. Wayne made room for them next to him.

"We're too tired to make plans, but we need to decide on some basics," Wayne said.

"Sure, that's fine. Honestly, I don't know if I can sleep. If you hear me pacing during the night please ignore it," Scott said.

"It'll take a while before any of us can rest," Annie said.

"I need to know if Alex made any requests about his funeral. Does he prefer to be embalmed or cremated?" Wayne asked.

"He didn't say," Scott said. "I believe Alex would want to be buried in Hallton. That is, if there are no local laws against embalming people with AIDS. Alex told me once that sometimes that's the case."

Wayne made a note. "I'll give a quick call to the funeral home now, and we'll finalize the rest tomorrow. Scott, we want you to plan as much of the service as you want."

"I'd like that." Scott looked around the kitchen. "Ooh, pie. I could use the sugar rush."

"Let me get it for you." Brian got up to get a plate. "I'm really going to miss Uncle Alex—and you. Could we come to Atlanta?"

"Absolutely," Scott said. "Gosh, I'm going to miss all of you. I think I've lost five pounds from playing basketball with Ben for the last two weeks. I need him for the other ten pounds."

Everyone laughed.

"Maybe we can drive down at the end of the summer before school starts," Annie said.

"I'd love for you to come. I'm thinking about having some sort of memorial service and everyone is invited—that means you, too, Jett." Scott smiled as he took a forkful of pie to his mouth, thinking of Alex. "You know Alex could eat more sweets than anyone I ever knew. I can't tell you the number of times he got up at night to get ice cream."

"He was like that as a child. Mom would bake a cake or pie and Alex would inhale it. After we'd go to bed, he'd sneak back to indulge," Annie said. "His favorite was peach pie."

"Peach everything," Scott laughed. "Peach ice cream, cobbler, peaches over ice cream—his office was painted peach. In the summer we'd go to the orchard to pick peaches. A few years ago he learned to can and freeze so he'd have his peaches all year round. He was obsessed."

"He was always learning something new. When we were kids he had this fascination with Evel Knievel. Remember?" Jett said.

Wayne nodded, "That was our Alex."

"Who is he?" Brian asked.

"This guy jumped cars, canyons, whatever with his motorcycle—a lot like Ben. Well, Alex never had a motorcycle, but he had a bike," Jett began.

A knock came at the front door.

"Go right ahead with your story. I'll see who it is." Wayne was remembering when Alex had tried to jump from the roof of one building to another with his bike to disastrous results.

Wayne got up from the table as Jett continued. He walked into the living room and saw a stately man at the front door. Wayne turned on the porch light.

"I am looking for the home of Wayne and Annie Whitley," asked the man.

"I'm Wayne Whitley. May I help you?"

"My name is Samuel Phillips, and I understand my son, Scott, is staying here."

Wayne opened the screen door.

"Come in, please. Phillips? Samuel Phillips, the preacher? You're Scott's father?" Wayne had watched him on satellite for years.

"Yes, I am. Scott left a message with my secretary this morning. May I see him if he's here?"

A peal of laughter rang from the kitchen.

"My brother-in-law died this afternoon and we're remembering him. Please, have a seat and I'll get Scott."

Samuel remained standing with his heart beating rapidly. He had been in a dream state since Esther made contact with him. Scott calling had made his life complete.

Wayne walked into the kitchen. "You have a guest in the living room."

Scott stood up. "Who could it possibly be?"

"Go on, you'll see."

Wayne motioned for Annie to begin her story again. Scott rounded the area to the living room and stopped. There stood a man who looked like his father but was much older.

"Son, please forgive me." Samuel walked over to Scott and embraced him.

℮ ℮ ℮

Their first moment together was emotional for both men.

Wayne told everyone in the kitchen that Scott's father was in the living room. Jett had met Samuel years before when he was playing football. He'd never considered the possibility that the same Scott visiting Annie and Wayne was the son of Samuel Phillips. For all the years of pain, God had worked miracles of restoration this day.

By bedtime, Ben was home and had shifted to the downstairs bedroom with Brian. Samuel and Scott were situated in the boys' room. The two men sat on their twin beds and faced each other. Sleep would not come until the wee hours of the morning. They had been talking about Samuel's mission trip when he began to tell Scott about recent events at the church.

"Resigned? From what I understand your ministry's unsinkable."

Scott sat back on the bed. Although he had never watched the ministry's TV program, he would periodically read about his famous father.

"The unsinkable sank and I'm out of favor. Something happened to me when I presented my intention to go on a mission. God jolted me from my complacency and opened my eyes to issues I've avoided for years." Samuel looked away from his son. "I had to face what I had done to you."

"I was wrong, Dad," Scott said. "I'm sorry I didn't answer your letters. Over the last few days I've been thinking about everything—that day and other times—and I'm just as guilty of prolonging our problems through the years as you are."

"I was the adult; I should have made the first step. I put too many things that didn't matter before you."

Scott leaned toward to his father. "They *did* matter. You've truly been a minister called by God. I haven't wanted to admit it, but it's evident by what you've accomplished."

"Sins are more than X-rated motion pictures or liquor stores. I was a workaholic. Investing time in your life would have been investing in the eternal. God hit me between the eyes with a sledgehammer. Son, I was pitiful as a father and husband."

"Why didn't you call about Mom?" Scott had been thinking about her death all afternoon. There was a dichotomy beginning to brew in his soul: anger for not being called, but regret for never trying to contact his mother. His family issues had always been solely between him and his father.

"I have no excuse for not calling you. I convinced myself that it would hurt your mother if you refused to come see her. Can you ever forgive me?"

"I probably would have hung up if you had called," Scott said.

"She knew you loved her," Samuel said. "Her last words were to ask me to tell you how much she loved you."

Scott was overwhelmed and suddenly wished he had contacted her.

"Thank you for being so honest. We need to talk about mom—but later . . ." Scott hesitated and then said, "Dad, today I did something I said I'd never do: I asked Jesus to come into my heart."

Samuel was still, not wanting to distract Scott from his train of thought. Scott continued.

"In the last few weeks I've started to see things differently. Having these people—people in Hallton—receive me as one of their own. Every single one of them disagrees with my sexual orientation, but they love me anyway."

Scott took a deep breath.

"Dad, I own a newspaper for gays and lesbians: the only job I've ever had has been this newspaper and it's been my heart and soul. As a Christian, it would be wrong for me to print a lot of the content—the part that's malicious and critical toward Christians. I've got some decisions to make about my future."

"I can't tell you what you should do—I truly don't know. Wait on God and trust him to lead you," Samuel advised after a thoughtful pause. "But this I know: I love you and nothing will ever separate us again."

This time it was not a random religious phrase, but a father who loved his son.

The two men embraced.

28

HALLTON CEMETERY✦TUESDAY, JULY 5

A SMALL CROWD GATHERED at the cemetery. Most of the people who had been at the Whitley home on Sunday morning were standing with them now. In the calmness of the country burial site the birds sang and a gentle wind blew. Scott sat between his father and Annie. Annie held his hand. Wayne's arm was around Annie's shoulders. The finality of Alex's death was hard. Each was lost in his or her treasured memories.

"I'm reading from the Bible Alex used in college," Jett began. "A passage he had marked was Psalm 147, verse 3: *He heals the brokenhearted and binds up their wounds.*

"We remember Alex Marshall as a young man with zealousness for the Lord. When Alex left, no one pursued him to let him know the Lord never stopped loving him. There are others like Alex in this community: at our work, in our church, and even in our circle of family and friends. God wants to use us to heal their hearts."

Jett closed the Bible, drew a breath, and looked directly at the Whitleys. "That's what Wayne and Annie did, not only for Alex but for me. Once you made your decision, you never wavered, even though it wasn't popular and I was one of your biggest obstacles for a time. Thank you." After a taking a moment to compose himself, Jett continued.

"I'd like to open the rest of the service to anyone who would like to say something about Alex." Jett stepped back beside Calvin. The leaves rustled in the gentle summer breeze. Scott stood.

"Alex died in peace. Through Wayne and Annie's unselfish devotion to Jesus Christ and through the lives of people like Jett and Donna, and Harley and Kitty, my life has changed forever. I'm honored to have had this time with each of you."

Others remembered Alex. Some cried as they talked. Truman talked about Alex fighting a group of boys who had called Calvin names. Annie spoke about the night Alex gave his life to the Lord. His roommate from college gave compelling accounts of Alex's life with Community Challenge. After an hour, the stories ended and Samuel Phillips got to his feet. Most had heard about Scott's father and many had come by the house to meet him as well as say good-bye to Alex.

"I must thank everyone here for what you've done for me. God has given me a second chance with my son thanks to your unselfish sacrifice. God bless you." Samuel sat down.

Calvin came to the front to pray.

"Almighty Father, we thank you that your hand wasn't too short to bring back our brother from the place where he had run. Your mercy and grace kept Alex until we were ready to go after him. Let's be ever mindful of the ones who need our love. In the name above all names, I pray. Amen."

PART FIVE

❧ The Commitment ❧

It is not my ability, but my response to God's ability, that counts.

Corrie ten Boom

29

CHRISTIAN WOMEN'S CLUB MEETING
JUNE 1, 2007

ANNIE TOOK A QUICK LOOK at her watch. There were only minutes remaining, but she still needed to tell them about one more thing. Out of the corner of her eye Annie saw Wayne smiling at her. He gave a little nod when he caught her eye.

"While Alex's death is the end of the story of how our family was reunified over the years, so many people ask: did Scott do the right thing? 'Right' can mean different things to different people. We know Scott is committed to following Christ. Early on our family made an agreement that we would leave it to God to work out the details, not just with Scott but Jett, Harley, our friends the Linders.

"As you figure by now, Scott has became a part of our family. In August we drove to Atlanta for a memorial service for Alex where Jett gave the eulogy. Scott went on a Labor Day fishing trip with Harley and Jett. The men were becoming fast friends. Jett hadn't yet shared the information about The Coach being his father with anyone—not even Wayne and me, though he'd confirmed it with Harley's mother.

"By late fall it seemed as if we had found the answer to all of life's problems. God was truly moving us forward, but it was a tragic turn of events that made us realize our commitment was more than one summer's experience. It was for a lifetime.

EMORY UNIVERSITY AREA, ATLANTA
FRIDAY, OCTOBER 28, 1994

Jett felt a little silly visiting Scott on his eight-hour layover in Atlanta without calling in advance, but he had an urge to see him before going back to Hallton. It was easy to find the office after seeing it when he was down for the memorial service—it was in a transformed home located in a pricey residential area with huge yards lush with trees.

The young woman who greeted him at the desk was attractive and efficient.

"May I help you?" she said with a smile.

"I'm Jett Taylor. I'd like to visit with Scott for a few minutes, if that's possible."

"He's in a meeting, but I'll buzz him. Please have a seat." She picked up the phone.

e⁊ e⁊ e⁊

"Scott, you own, but *we run* a gay newspaper. In case you've forgotten this one—your baby—is our flagship paper that's marketed all over the Southeastern part of the United States. Here's the bottom line: unless you stop the conservative bit, we're going to start losing in a big way. Scott, you haven't been yourself since Alex died. I know how much he meant to you, and maybe you ought to see a counselor before..." Lesley decided it wouldn't be in good taste to continue down that road. "Well, you just don't need to lose anything else."

Scott had battled with Lesley each month since August when the figures came in.

"How are we looking, Lesley?" Scott tried to act as if he didn't know the sales were going south on the bottom line faster than the swallows migrate to Argentina this time of year.

"It's no surprise our ad revenues are down since you stopped the articles and censored the editorials against the right wing. These conservatives make our lives hell and you don't want to address the issues anymore. Is Mr. First Amendment Phillips getting squeamish? The bottom line is our Halloween edition is the second largest after Pride Week and our ad sales for that issue are lower than in 1985."

"I understand." Scott scanned the financial report.

"If you don't want to run this paper, I'll buy it," Lesley said. "I don't mean to be rude, but did you become born-again or something when you went to Wisconsin?"

Scott did not know what he was going to do about the paper, but today was not the day to reveal that indeed he had committed his life to Christ. The phone buzzed in the conference room as he was about to respond.

"Phillips here ... Sure, I'll be right out. Tell him not to leave." Scott looked at Lesley. "One of Alex's friends is here, and it's time for lunch. I promise I'll have a decision on Monday."

∾ ∾ ∾

Scott met Jett at the door to his office and they embraced liked long-lost friends. He introduced Jett to Lesley along with Lance, his star reporter, and Chris, the receptionist, before they went inside and closed the door.

"They look pretty close," Lesley commented as she stood at the receptionist's desk.

"Oh no, that's Jett Taylor," Lance said pointing toward the door. "He's an ultra-conservative Christian. I used to watch him play with the Giants. May I see you in your office?"

Lesley nodded and they walked to her office on the other side of the building.

Lesley sat at her desk and took a sip of water while Lance took a seat across from her. "Okay, what's the big story?"

"A friend sent me a newspaper from Austin, Texas. He thought there might be a connection between Samuel Phillips, that famous conservative preacher, and our own Scott."

Lance pulled a stiff, slightly yellowed copy of a newspaper from his brief-case. Lesley perused the article. There was a paragraph about Phillips having remorse over "Samuel Jr." leaving home fifteen years before.

"I don't think Scott *has* parents. He was put on Earth by a spaceship, and besides that his legal name is simply plain old Scott Phillips—that I know." Lesley threw the newspaper across the desk.

"You're letting your friendship get in the way of investigative reporting. This has to be our Scott. The date of this paper is around the time Alex died. Maybe it has something to do with the censoring of articles and editorials. You know that better than anyone because you get the phone calls from dis-gruntled advertisers who are demanding an explanation."

Lesley's brown eyes snapped up. She admired Scott's business ethics and would hate to see him suffer, but this information would be a huge scoop if it were proven. *Just imagine*, she thought, *the successful owner of most of the gay newspapers in the U.S. as the son of an equally successful Christian fundamental-ist preacher*. Lesley didn't want Scott to suffer the fallout of a revelation of this magnitude, but she felt a responsibility to their readers.

"Okay, make some calls. Don't tell anyone, and let me know what you find. He might be the Ice Man, but he always comes through when I need him. I don't want *anyone* to get wind of this before I have a chance to talk with him. Deal?"

"Deal."

Lance grabbed his newspaper and left the office. Lesley stared at her desk. If this was true, it would be difficult to keep a story like this under wraps for very long. However, she had invested a great deal in this newspaper, and she didn't want to lose it. Yes, Monday would be a good day to talk with Scott about the financial future of the paper.

❧ ❧ ❧

Jett and Scott settled into the back booth of the restaurant. Scott faced the door in case someone entered whom he did not want to overhear them talk-ing. The background music drowned out most of their conversation.

"This is what my dad would call an appointment from God," Scott began.

"How's your dad? We've exchanged letters over the last few months," Jett said.

"He's doing well—and due to arrive back in Austin late Monday afternoon," Scott said. "I intend to see him at Thanksgiving. We've agreed that it's time for me to come home and to directly confront what happened to us."

"When we were on the fishing trip you had just sent him that letter about your mother's death. I'm really sorry I haven't gotten back with you to find out his reaction. I went to visit my mom and got mired down in some old stuff. I didn't mean to forget you," Jett said.

"There have been many letters, and I'll start writing him as I'm thinking about certain issues, and before I know it I'm boiling mad. I mail it, regret it, and then call him to apologize. It's been difficult," Scott said. "You know what bothers me the most? That in all those years I was angry with Dad, not once—I mean for one minute—did I think about what I was doing to Mom. She probably died thinking she was a terrible mother. That was unfair to her; I hurt her as deeply as Dad did."

"Your father is trying—he's told me many times in the letters he sends," Jett said.

"I never could imagine us being at this place in our relationship, even if I hadn't left home. Dad is so different now. I know it's going to eventually smooth out, because my angry days are coming fewer and farther between," Scott said, and then asked, "How are things in Hallton?"

"Great. Our new church is growing. Clark's direction has been great help for people to get through the rough places without shame."

"Sounds like a place I need. I've tried the suburban churches because I'm not as well-known outside the perimeter of the city. I'm accepted until I open up just to say I'm gay, and then they try to push me into an ex-gay ministry. Their claim of friendship is exposed as an agenda to make me straight. I need friends who'll fish with me or come by for a surprise lunch." Scott raised his fork and smiled as he pointed it toward Jett. "I believe with support from Christians like you and Harley, I could be stronger and know what I need to do with my life."

Jet's smile was quickly replaced by a questioning look.

"Let's backtrack: I'm not so sure I understand the term 'ex-gay ministry'—I can surmise the general idea, but I don't remember having them in our neck of the woods," Jett replied.

"The concept is that we're not born gay, but instead being gay is a sub-conscious choice based on variables like an absent father, being molested, poor self-image—you get the drift."

Jett nodded.

"Actually, the research I've found shows the programs have marginal success; however, because I live in the South ..." Scott gave a weary sigh and started again. "By living in the South, there's a great deal of pressure to change our orientation, and these faith-based programs are seen as the vehicle to make that change possible."

Jett studied Scott for a moment before he spoke. His voice resonated with both compassion as well as concern.

"Have you ever felt we didn't accept you?" Jett asked.

"Everyone in Hallton has accepted me unconditionally. I've never felt any pressure to change," Scott said, and then he continued with some hesitation. "I honestly don't see how I could love another man; Alex was everything to me."

"Of course you miss Alex. If Harley were to die, I'd be devastated. It would take a very long time to get over it. I'm talking years—maybe never," Jett said.

Scott paused briefly before changing the subject. "More than finding a church, I've got a business problem. Since July I've stopped my attacks on the religious right, and as a result our advertisements have dropped significantly. I either need to follow the conservative path all the way or go back to the way I used to conduct business. There doesn't seem to be any middle ground on this issue."

"You obviously have a great business mind. You survived the stock market crash in 1987, and that says a lot. God prospers a business."

"I have a hard time believing God looks favorably on what I do for a living," Scott replied.

"Maybe you need to tweak your approach a little bit; change the direction. If you continue as you're going what does that mean in terms of the newspaper?"

"Jett, my concern is for my staff, because part of the perks is profit sharing. It affects their income when I make these editorial changes," Scott replied. "I probably should have sold the paper a couple of months ago, but I kept putting it off."

"Do you have a buyer?" Jett asked.

"My CFO expressed an interest just today."

"Maybe God is giving you an escape. Whatever you decide, we're here to support you. You've got a home in Hallton if you need a place to go."

"Hallton is a special place, and I might live there someday, but not now," Scott replied.

Jett took a bite of his salad and hesitated before he spoke again. "Let me throw this out to you. What about girls? Would you consider dating women?"

Scott answered, "There was a time just before I entered high school when I had girlfriends. If I decided to date girls again, my concern is I don't know if there's any girl who can please me both physically and emotionally. But I do worry about being alone."

"Many widows and widowers live the rest of their lives without physical intimacy," Jett replied. "Scott, there's a myth propagated by the media that a spouse is to be everything to us, and mad passion is to evolve each time you look into the other person's eyes. I would be nothing without my wife, but that doesn't mean she fulfills my every hope and dream—no person can do that—only God can."

"I like Donna," Scott said. "Not to change the subject, but how did you meet her?"

"By accident really: she lived in a small town outside of Meridian, Mississippi, after she returned from Kenya with her missionary parents. Donna was a public school teacher and had a little group of boys in middle school who were almost out of control. She didn't know football but had heard them talk about me. I was going to be in Birmingham to sign autographs at an athletic shoe endorsement. On a whim she brought these dozen young boys to the store in the church van."

"Wow, that's a story that puts a smile on your face. Was it love at first sight?" Scott asked.

"I was intrigued by her, but my heart was barely over Rita's death enough to think about another girl. It was all about the kids in the beginning. I decided to send her tickets for the kids for the Giants game against the New Orleans Saints . . ."

"And *then* you fell in love?" Scott asked with excitement. "I'm not usually into how people meet, but I feel comfortable enough with you to ask anything, I think."

"I started noticing her more after the game when we had dinner with the kids. Then several months later Donna and her school put together a recognition day for me, figuring they'd just send me a scrapbook of the event. I managed to get there without any press finding out. That day changed my life. I was with a group of poor, troubled kids, and I totally understood because I was just like them when I was that age.

"I could identify with them and was able to make an impact when I spoke from my heart. Those dozen boys—now men—still stay in touch. We're planning a trip down there for Thanksgiving. They said they want to give back to me now." Jett stopped and smiled. "Isn't that incredible how God will take a terrible situation and have people there to hold you when you need to be picked up?

"Anyway, back to Donna: after spending the day at the school, I asked her out to dinner. And we slowly started a relationship and fell in love. Donna's love accepts me for who I am, what I've done, and she has always been there to restore my heart. When it happens for you, you'll just know."

"*Just know*—thanks," Scott said with a little chuckle. Then he got serious again. "You spoke of the myth—so what's the other part of the myth?"

"That part is that love means never-ending sex. Scott, sex is a natural response to what is felt in the heart. The passion from lust can only be temporarily satisfied. Harley's marriage almost ended because of lust," Jett responded.

"They're so happy now. I guess God can work miracles even today," Scott said and then shifted so he could talk more honestly. "Jett, I constantly wonder: what if Alex had lived, what would I have done?" Scott said.

"Everyone has 'what ifs'—certainly I've had more than my share lately," Jett said. "What if I had listened to Alex that night when he came to my hotel room in Green Bay with that warning from God? Rita would be alive and possibly Alex wouldn't have gone to Atlanta. If that had happened, where would you be? That's why God is God, and you have to trust him."

"Trusting is difficult for me," Scott replied.

"I think that trusting God is difficult for everyone at some point in their lives. As time goes by I think you'll get a clearer picture of what you need to do. I find it's happening that way for me."

"I hope so. So tell me, what brings you to Atlanta?" Scott crunched into his nachos.

"Last night I was in Miami, selling my sporting goods franchise—inked the deal and got the check. Selling my business gives me time to pursue what's in my heart. Actually, once I realized that I had time, I decided I'd come in person to town to tell you I took your advice. You and Harley were right. Now that I've finished dealing with my mom, I'm free to go see Rita's parents and apologize."

"Wow. That's a big step. Are they expecting you?" Scott asked as he took a bite of salad.

"No, I'm afraid they'd refuse to see me if I announced myself first. It's time they know. I let her dad assume all the blame. He felt he'd pushed her too hard in school. Anyway, once I get back, then I'm going to follow whatever path God has for me."

"Is Donna going with you?"

"We both felt I needed to do this in person, but alone. It's a short trip to Pittsburg, and I'll be home by the time Will is ready for bed," Jett said.

"Well, Monday will be my day, too. If you have time could we run over some ideas for my business before you head out?" Scott asked.

"I've got four hours before I need to head down to the airport. Sure, it would be my pleasure, but you're the one with the business skills," Jett laughed. "How many people start a successful business from their college dorm?"

"You give me confidence, old buddy," Scott smiled as they continued to talk.

30

TAYLOR HOME⌇THE NEXT NIGHT,
SATURDAY, OCTOBER 29, 1994

"YOUR TURN," JETT SAID, as he grabbed the ball.

Harley and Jett had been playing football for two hours. They would name a play from an old game and then pass the ball like they did in their glory years.

"Legion Field, 1977, Alabama vs. Ole Miss: second quarter, fourth and goal." Jett handed the ball off to Harley, who ran to an imaginary goal.

Ella Hamilton watched them from the deck for a moment before she had to call them in. Jett had gone to see Ella the week after Alex's death, and they chose this day to talk to others. Ella was there for Jett when his own mom, Rainey, could not come through—it had been the end of September before Rainey agreed to talk about The Coach. Even then she focused on the great shame Jett's birth brought her, and immediately it transferred to Jett as rejection.

"Boys, time to come in," Ella yelled out to the lawn. She was proud of the way Jett had grown so much these last few months. She considered him her second son.

Harley heard her and shouted back. "Just a minute, Mom, we've got one more play."

"One more and that's all," Ella replied.

"Okay, Mom." Harley waved then turned back to Jett. "You heard her. Last play and it's your turn to call."

"September 4, 1962. This time you receive the pass."

Harley walked over to Jett. "What did you say?"

"This is the last ball, so you get over there before your mom is out here again."

Jett steadied himself and threw. The ball sailed through the air straight into Harley's hands. He was headed for an imaginary goal when Jett tackled him. The two men went down and rolled across the grass.

"Since when do you tackle?" Harley laughed. "Man, I'm too old for this."

"I have to tell you something." Jett had a serious tenor as he spoke. "September 4, 1962, was the best day of my life. That was the day I met you. You've meant everything to me. Because of you, I am who I am."

"I did nothing for you that any friend wouldn't have done." Harley propped himself up by one leg and punched Jett on the shoulder.

"I've thought this all my life, but I never told you. I've been rehearsing all the way back from Atlanta what I'd say to you because it's so important," Jett said.

"There you were, the smartest kid in town, with everything and *you let me* be your friend. I had so much trouble reading in first grade, but you taught me how, and no one ever knew. There wasn't a day in our lives when you ever acted like you were reluctant to be my friend."

"Not be your friend? Jett, you're the reason I played football." Harley smiled. "You're the best friend I've ever had."

"The day I took you back to prison, I was scared I'd lose you and never be able to tell you these things." Jett cleared his throat and continued. "Please, remember how indebted I am. This summer you made me be accountable for my sins, Harley. Since then you've taught me what it is to be a real man—not like The Coach said a man was, but a man who is humble and vulnerable. You taught me how to be a good father—like you—and love my son the way a boy should be loved."

Harley pulled Jett toward him in a neck hold. "If anyone should be talking about how important that day was in 1962, it's me. Through the years—

so many things, Jett: you have no idea, but you saved my life the day you took me back to prison. I heard that The Coach advised you to turn your back on me, but you bucked him. It was difficult for you to act against him; I know that. I'm so thankful for what you've done."

As they reminisced, they were reminded of the time they sank Tom's boat on a fishing trip, and it made them laugh. Ella appeared on the deck again and their conversation ended long before they were ready.

When they got into the house the people had gathered. Jett walked into the laundry room and took off his sweater and placed it on the dryer. By the time he entered the den, everyone was seated. Ella sat on the hearth next to Harley. A very pregnant Kitty had the recliner. The people who had helped Annie and Wayne during Alex's illness, like Truman, were there to help give Jett answers. Finally, Jett motioned for Ella to begin, and he took a seat on the floor in front of Donna.

"Before Alex died, Jett made a promise to him to clear up some of the questions about The Coach." Ella stopped for a moment. "The old-timers here remember when Bill Marshall was a joy. He was wonderful with kids and a good leader. Things changed, and most of us thought Bill's disappointment with Alex contributed to his change. As the years progressed, Bill became so rigid that he had no life, and he wasn't kind to our children." Ella touched Harley's hand.

"From the little that Jett and I know, the root of Bill's problem was a secret he was hiding, coupled with his inability to repent. However, before I go any further, I need to repent. I can't talk about Bill Marshall's issues without correcting my own first." Ella put her arm around Harley's neck.

"Everyone here knows how angry I was with Harley after Tom died." Ella swallowed hard. "I'm profoundly sorry. Tom always said you'd be the best husband and father and you are. Forgive me." She kissed him.

"Praise God," Susan said. "He needs this, Ella."

Jett was elated. This would bring healing to Harley. Donna was the first to speak.

"Thanks, Ella. I need to confess, too, Harley. For many years I couldn't understand what Jett saw in you, and I even encouraged Kitty to divorce you. After your conversion, Jett began bringing home these wonderful reports from his visits to see you in prison. In this last year I've come to see why my husband has always been so completely devoted to you. You're an incredible man, Harley."

"Thanks, Donna." Harley turned back to Ella. "Mom, this isn't necessary."

"Yes, it is," Ella said as she embraced her son.

"Harley, in one of our last talks Alex said to tell you that the information we're about to reveal is what your mom confronted The Coach with the day she came to school," Jett said.

Harley was about to say something to his mother when Ella interrupted.

"The Coach had been setting you up for years because he didn't like your dad. I was worried about what might happen with the rest of the school year," Ella said. "I needed to make sure Bill was kept in line, and I told Bill if he hit you one more time, I'd tell Jett his secret. Bill called me names. I told him not to push, because I'd take him before the board of education in a heartbeat. It was one tough old bird against another, and this tough bird meant to win."

Harley smiled. "Why didn't you tell me what you did?"

"Tom didn't even know I confronted Bill. Your father thought everyone could be handled with kindness, but I didn't have time to test the waters. I knew what it would take to hold his feet to the fire—and it turned out to be a win-win situation." Ella gave a little wink and a smile as she finished.

Jett opened the books on The Coach. He was devastated by the reality that The Coach only wanted the fame, instead of recognizing him as a son. Tonight was a time to have these things explained and, hopefully, healed.

"I made a promise to Alex to get in touch with Ella and work through the issues about The Coach. This morning we met with Annie and Wayne, and tonight I wanted to lay out the information for your input." Jett motioned for Ella to speak.

"Rainey couldn't be here because the shame is still too great," Ella said. "Let me start with how I came to know Bill Marshall's most guarded secret. We were at a baseball field. It was one of those terrible days when Bill was screaming at Alex for striking out."

Annie nodded at the memory of all those ball games that were agony to watch. The Coach was a man of many moods and personalities. Ella's and Jett's revelations explained so much.

"When Bill went back into the stands, he sat next to Rainey and started to proposition her without realizing who she was. I overheard the whole thing," Ella said.

"That man," Truman said. "He had an eye for the ladies. I'm sorry, Annie. Your mama knew about the other women, and they never had any sort of peace in their marriage because of it. I must say that after he gave his life to Christ, he never had another woman."

The Coach considered Truman his closest friend. Truman was a plain-spoken man of the soil who lived a simple life committed to Christ.

"Rainey was upset and blurted out information about her life," Ella said. "She was a teenager in Hallton and went by her given name Lorraine. The coach didn't recognize her because she'd changed her hairstyle and filled out. She used to hang out and watch evening football practice—like every other girl she was infatuated with the handsome, charismatic coach. One evening Bill took her home and, as usual, her parents were out."

Harley looked up. "Jett, are you The Coach's son?"

"I couldn't tell you until we had told Annie. It's been hard to accept, because I begged him to be my father but he never admitted to it. He didn't want to fall off that pedestal everyone—including me—had him up on, I guess."

Donna spoke carefully. "This has crushed Jett's heart more than any of you can ever imagine. We really need everyone's input."

"Bill used some slick moves to get into her house, and by the time he went home, Rainey was pregnant." Ella motioned for Jett to move closer to her. "Bill never knew she was pregnant."

"When she told her parents, they disowned her and sent her to live with her grandmother in another state. When Jett was about to start grade school, Rainey moved back to Hallton to a little shack out beyond Fetter's Market. Their living conditions were deplorable. I didn't want to leave Jett the first evening I took him home. Harley remembers how I worried."

Harley slid down to the floor next to Jett and put his arm around him. Tonight Jett felt as vulnerable as he was when he was a little boy.

"Rainey worked in the dry cleaners as a seamstress. I talked with the owner but found out Rainey wouldn't accept charity—he had tried to help her. Her family had taught her very little, but one thing she learned was false pride. She'd starve or freeze before taking any money—which meant Jett starved and froze, too. Tom and I did everything we could to make things happen naturally so Rainey wouldn't be suspicious," Ella added.

"If it hadn't been for your family I'd have lost hope. I never knew what unconditional love meant until I knew you," Jett said.

"When I got home from the ballpark after overhearing Rainey that night I told Tom that Bill was Jett's real father. He went to see Bill," Ella said. "Bill denied knowing Jett's mom and ordered Tom off his property."

"This next thing is difficult to discuss," Jett said. "When I was ten I stole something from a grocery store. This was the day Alex found out I was The Coach's son," Jett said. "Mom had given Tom the authority to handle me, because I was becoming unruly. On this day it was different. He wept and apologized for not taking better care of my mother and me. However, Alex told me that your dad went over to their house and told The Coach he had to start taking care of me."

Jett thought for a minute before continuing. "The Coach took me under his wing with football, but he never offered to buy me anything as simple as a soda. On the other hand, Tom bought a house and rented it to my mother— all the rent money was given to me when I went to college. He gave Mom a good job at the bank."

"Bill was always coming over whenever he had any sort of big problem, and that night he was frantic," Truman said. "He paced like a wild animal. I told him that whatever it was, he needed to confess his sin and do something to correct it. Hiding the 'problem' would only lead to trouble. He didn't mention it again for years."

"About the time you boys turned fifteen, I asked Bill about this 'problem' he had always talked about. After I guessed his sin, he finally told me that Jett was his boy. Bill said he was taking 'care of him.' I told him, 'No, someone else takes care of him. Only you take the credit for his God-given talent. Repent and make it right. Otherwise one day you'll look in the mirror and won't remember who Bill Marshall was.' He was afraid what people would say even though Jett was everything he wanted in a son. He just couldn't risk sacrificing so much, like you said, Jett. When Bill walked off that day, he walked off from God."

Annie looked at her brother and was tender as well as sincere. "I've thought about this all afternoon. As much as he could love anyone, he loved you."

Jett stared into the carpet. Wayne picked up the conversation.

"We're excited to know that you're Annie's blood brother. It's the best news we've heard in months. Everyone in this room knows The Coach knew nothing about love. When he refused to acknowledge his adultery, he lost the most cherished possession he could ever have: a father-son relationship with you."

"Did Bill ever call you 'son' during his last days? Or did he ever imply that you were his son?" Susan asked.

"Never. The day he died I told him he had been like a father to me. He just looked away and said nothing," Jett replied.

"It's so strange." Susan shook her head. "When I visited him a couple of days before he died, he called you his son. I thought he was on too much medication. Even on his deathbed he was unable to acknowledge you. I'm so sorry. I don't mean to make this harder. We've all been disappointed by Bill Marshall through the years."

"Harley always told me something was wrong with The Coach's legalism. In my need for a father I overlooked The Coach's obvious failings."

"I have a story, and I think it might help you and your real brother," Truman said.

"You mean Harley?" Jett asked, with a slight chuckle.

"God put you in the family he wanted you in." Truman smiled as he spoke. "I've never seen people love a child as much as Tom and Ella loved you. The first time I saw you, Tom had you in his arms showing you off. You completed their family. Harley's your brother—not by blood, but by God giving you to their family. Listen to me, son."

Truman spoke softly. "After Bill died I was in the bank and Tom motioned for me to come in his office to talk. I saw the photos of his family, and smack-dab in the middle was you, Jett. Tom said to me, 'I'd have given anything to have adopted him. My one regret in life is that I couldn't give Jett my name.'"

Truman walked over to Jett and squatted down to look at him face-to-face. He put his large hand on Jett's shoulder. Here was a man of the earth working to restore Jett's heart. The words he had already spoken were healing.

"Bill loved you, but when you got Rita pregnant, you couldn't let him know or he'd have turned his back on you. Alex was a good boy, and we know how terrible Bill was to him. Tom loved Harley and believed in him through thick and thin, and nothing could stop Tom from loving his son. God is that kind of father. You've always known Tom Hamilton as your father. If you ever call anyone 'Daddy,' it should be Tom, because he called you his son."

Jett's longing for a father ended with those words.

31

EUBANKS HOME, AUSTIN

Even though the house was built on a concrete slab, the floors cracked and groaned as Eubanks hefted his weight around the house. He carried two cups of tea, splashing with each uneven step. While most people went home and relaxed, this man remained dressed in a starched shirt, business trousers, and tie.

The modest house had ordinary decorations. Everything was in its place, as if it needed to pass the most rigid white-glove test. Gerald Eubanks ruled his home with little compassion. Whatever love that once passed between him and his wife disappeared long ago. Mayzelle had developed an ever-watchful eye that made sure this pitiless man was pleased.

The Eubanks had few friends who were not church members. The guest of the evening could hardly be called a friend. Brent was an opportunist who had repeatedly used Eubanks—most recently to uncover the domestic-violence shelter where his family had been sent. Now that they were home, Brent decided to spend time making sure no one ever helped his wife again.

"We hope that you and your family will be able to come by after the harvest festival at church on Monday night. We'll have a few little treats for your kids," Eubanks said as he handed Brent a cup of tea.

"That sounds like a wonderful idea, Gerald. Our family has been renewed thanks to your effort." Brent sounded convincing.

"Thank you very much," Eubanks gushed.

In addition to being the administrative pastor, Eubanks had taught the men's Bible class for thirty years. His class topic was being the head of the household, and he had little regard for women. To Eubanks, women were the weaker sex, easily deceived, foolish, and best when controlled.

It upset him that Samuel Phillips never fully accepted his biblical view. If he had understood that men were to rule over their homes, then Samuel would never have sent Brent's family to a domestic-violence shelter. Over the last few months Eubanks had been able to bring their church back around to a course where everyone understood God's order for the family.

"Candace's Jezebel ways originated when that preacher Phillips started telling her it's okay to leave me by going to some kind of safe house that's totally against God's plan for a family. I was the victim, Gerald," Brent said.

He wanted the words to rekindle Eubanks's holy war against Samuel Phillips. There was information floating around that Samuel Phillips would be returning to Austin in the next few days, and Brent was determined that this preacher would not interfere in his life again.

"God will judge Samuel—you rest assured it's going to happen, and happen very soon, I believe. I wouldn't be surprised if God didn't strike him down, along with that reprobate son of his. Scott is incapable of true repentance. Trust me, judgment will come soon."

Eubanks took the remote and clicked on the television.

"It won't be too soon for me," Brent said.

There was no further need to discuss Brent's wife. Various women were teaching her how to be a proper Christian wife. Eubanks heard that Candace was resistant at first but over the weeks had repented for leaving her husband.

This should end any thoughts the other women had of leaving their husbands. Eubanks had taken care of that when he handpicked their new pastor. There would be no more problems with people having a divided heart between Samuel's new way of thinking and the way of the Bible.

TAYLOR HOME

"Thanks for coming," Jett said as he gave Kitty a hug. He waited until she had gotten into the car and closed her door, and then he looked across the top of the car at Harley who hadn't yet opened his door. The cold late fall wind had begun to pick up. He noticed that Harley was hesitating.

"You plan on taking a smoke before you get into the car?" Jett asked. "If so I'll stand out here and talk with you."

"No, I've decided to give them up. I've thought about it for a while, but our game tonight showed me that I need to do it if I plan to outlive you," Harley joked as he tossed his almost empty pack to Jett. "Throw these away so I won't be tempted."

"I'm proud of you," Jett replied.

"You keep improving, so I've got to find some way to keep up," Harley laughed. Then he walked over to Jett and gave him a big bear hug. "Little brother."

Jett watched them drive away before he went inside. He found Donna in the kitchen, and she began speaking as he dropped the crushed pack into the garbage.

"Truman was right. Tom loved you so much." Donna walked over to him and put her arms around his waist.

"Have I told you today that my heart has been restored by your deep love for me?" Jett kissed her. "And I plan to spend everyday for the rest of my life making up to you for all the times I let you down."

"Jett, you're exactly the man I always saw you as. I can't ask for anything else—except a backrub—you think maybe?" Donna smiled.

"Sure, let me check on Will, and I'll be right there," Jett said as he gave her a kiss and headed down the hall toward their son's room. He covered his son, who roused a little.

"Hey, buddy." Jett kissed him. "Go back to sleep and tomorrow we'll have some fun."

It had been a long time since Jett looked forward to what the future might bring. His mind was exploding with ideas to bless his family. Jett was very thankful for all he had been given as well as for what had been restored.

32

ATLANTA⁓MONDAY MORNING, OCTOBER 31

SCOTT'S FRIEND KERRY BRENNAN had been released from the hospital after his first opportunistic infection with AIDS. It was painful for Scott to be around anyone with AIDS. If it hadn't been for their long friendship, Scott would have gladly distanced himself from anyone with the disease—not just now but for the rest of his life.

"I don't care about going to a party," Scott said to him over the phone. "Why don't I just bring over some dinner and we can watch television? You think about it and I'll call later."

Scott hung up as his staff arrived. He got up from his desk and walked into the waiting area. Chris was returning from the kitchen with a cup of coffee.

"Good coffee, Scott. For a guy who doesn't drink it, you make the best I've ever had," she said.

"Thanks. The little Colombian bean picker on television taught me." Scott smiled. "Will you have Lesley come in as soon as she gets here?"

"Sure." Chris sat down and began her work.

Scott went back into his office and thought about his phone call. Kerry's idea of going to a party might not be a bad one. Scott could test the waters of being single again in his community before he decided if he wanted to sell the paper.

He pulled the figures out of the top desk drawer. His talk with Jett had been a tremendous help. Jett advised a clean break, plus additional time for the new owners to relocate their offices. Scott could then use the house for another business or sell it for a hefty profit. Still, Scott didn't like the idea of having the newspaper in existence if he couldn't manage it.

Another hour passed before Chris stuck her head in the door. "Lesley called. She has a virus and said she'll see you tomorrow."

"Thank you," Scott said.

He picked up the phone to tell Kerry they would go out. Scott would attempt to make his old life work one last time before giving it all to God.

TUESDAY, 1:45 A.M.

Scott pulled his Jeep into the driveway of the home he and Alex had shared. He felt sick. It was not Lesley's virus, although he wished it were. The party had been only marginally entertaining. At first he thought his malaise was because Alex was gone, but soon he realized the entire scene held no significance for him. On the way home Kerry had gotten sick, and Scott stayed with him until he was stable. It was difficult knowing that Kerry would soon be a name on a granite stone.

Scott felt like he was in the middle of a crevasse. On one side was his life of the last two decades, but Alex was gone, the newspaper was in a crisis, and he had no interest in meeting another man. On the other hand, if he walked away from the gay community, he would leave everything: friends, business acquaintances, and the places familiar to him. There was the uncertainty of a straight relationship. If he found a woman who would accept him, could he be a committed husband? Did he really want to be with a woman?

Questions hung around his neck like a noose. Everything felt wrong. When he entered the house he noticed his answering machine had eight messages; he rarely received one call at home a week. He unplugged the phones without reviewing his calls and fell into a fitful sleep. In a few hours he would have to confront Lesley about the business.

33

LESLEY'S OFFICE ❧ 8:30 A.M.

"HERE'S WHAT YOU WANTED, and it's just as I suspected." Lance sat before Lesley with the information and began reading from his notes: "Dr. Samuel Phillips was the senior pastor of the largest church in the Southwest. He had, according to quotes from members of his congregation, 'offered unsound biblical advice to a married woman.' Actually what happened was Dr. Phillips sent a married woman to a domestic-violence shelter after he found that her husband had beaten her. This, however, went against the church doctrine and Phillips resigned—some people say he was forced out. In his last sermon, he expressed regret about being a terrible father to his son, Scott, who hadn't been home in fifteen years," Lance finished.

Lesley still had mixed emotions about presenting the fact of their knowledge to Scott, but if he did not come around to her way of doing business, it might be necessary. "Don't tell anyone about this until I talk with Scott. He must really hate his old man if he's never told anyone about him."

Lance opened the door and heard Scott talking to Chris.

"I'll go see him now," Lesley said, picking up the financial reports and tucking Lance's information in the middle.

"I need to speak to him first," Lance said.

They walked past the kitchen and the smaller offices into the reception area. As they passed Chris, Lesley asked that she hold Scott's calls. Scott was sipping his morning glass of tea as Lesley walked into his office. "We need to talk."

Lance came in behind Lesley, eating an apple from the basket on Chris's desk. "Scott, I'm so sorry about your friend."

Scott looked up with a puzzled expression. "What friend?"

"The football player: Jett Taylor. I know it's a shock."

"What's a shock?" Scott's face plainly said that he had no clue.

"You haven't heard about the crash?" Lesley asked.

Scott cautiously shook his head as Lance cut back in.

"Your friend was on the plane that crashed late yesterday afternoon, Scott. I'm afraid Jett Taylor is dead," Lance said tenderly.

Scott felt like he was in slow motion. "Say again: plane crash?"

"The plane was on its way to Chicago from Pittsburgh. It blew up somewhere over Indiana, and there were no survivors." Lance said each word distinctly.

"He wasn't going to Indiana. It's a mistake," Scott contended.

"Scott, it blew up over Indiana—it took off from Pittsburgh. Watch this." Lance grabbed the remote control from Scott's desk and snapped on the television. *The Today Show* was on and it was the half hour. "It's the lead story on the news."

The horror unfolded before Scott's eyes. First the anchor read the news, and then they cut to an aerial view of the wreckage. The cameras cut back to a picture of Jett, and the anchor concluded the story with a brief overview of Jett's life: Heisman Trophy winner, NFL Hall of Fame quarterback. There was no question, Jett was on that flight.

Sick and pale, Scott said, "I need to be alone. Close the door, please."

His hand shook when he pressed the speed dial. On the second ring Wayne answered.

"How can it be true?" Scott said without first saying hello; his voice broke on the last word.

"We tried to call you last night. Losing Jett is inconceivable. All we've done is hold each other and cry. Please come up, Scott. You need to be with family."

"I saw him Friday," Scott said.

"He told me," Wayne said. "I talked with your dad last night after he heard the news on CNN. He'll be leaving Austin midday to come up here."

Scott was able to get his voice under control.

"I'll call Dad. If I can't get there by this evening, you'll see me tomorrow."

"We have room for both of you, so plan on staying with us," Wayne said.

"Your place is home, Wayne," Scott said. "I'll get back with you to give you arrival details."

Scott hung up the phone and called his father.

34

GRAVESIDE ~ SUNDAY, NOVEMBER 6

"Now comes the time that we give him back to you, Lord—Jett, why did you have to die?" Harley struggled with the prayer to end the graveside service. He held Jett's son, who sobbed into his shoulder.

Scott was all too familiar with Harley's pain. He stood beside his father as the citizens of Hallton laid Jett to rest. An early winter snow blew as the wind billowed up under their newly purchased topcoats. They only wanted to ease their unspeakable grief and find a reason for this senseless death. Across from Scott were the dozen African American men from Mississippi who had been in Donna's middle school class long ago. They had traveled all this way to lay their hero to rest. Jett had become Scott's hero, too, in recent months. How could this have happened?

This had been the longest week of Scott's life. He met his father in Chicago and they drove to Hallton. The next morning they went to see Jett's widow,

Donna. At the Taylor home, they did not wait long before a gracious woman answered the door and extended her hand to Samuel.

"Come in, gentlemen. My husband and Donna are in the kitchen. I'm Lucy, Donna's mother."

Lucy led them through the hallway. Scott saw Donna sitting at the table crying. Her father and Kitty were comforting her. Donna's right hand held a piece of paper that had come out of the envelope lying beneath her shaking fingertips.

"Donna, baby girl, some people are heartless." The man stroked her hair.

"It would be wise to let your dad open your mail for a while," Kitty said. "Are you sure you don't want a sedative? I think you need something." She was one of the few physicians left in this area, because most had moved on to the city where they could make more money.

Donna's father motioned for them to be seated.

"I'm Henry. Thanks so much for coming." He shook their hands. "We're working through an unfortunate situation. Donna received a letter that condemned Jett's recent problems."

Henry sat down again and put his arm around her. Samuel sat next to Henry. Scott noticed Harley sitting alone on the deck.

"May I see the note?" asked Samuel.

The pompous edge was gone. Scott watched his father as Donna handed him the note. Samuel bit his bottom lip as he read. The writer stated that God had ordained Jett's death and that he deserved to die because he had taken the life of an innocent child when he forced his girlfriend to have an abortion. And that was why Jett and Donna had had so many miscarriages. The writer was obviously someone who knew them.

"There will always be people who cause hurt," Samuel said, pulling a chair close to Donna. "The person who penned this letter is wrong. Remember how wonderful Jett was." He balled up the note and put it in Donna's hand. "Kitty is right—this is garbage."

As Donna cried and the two men comforted her, Scott turned back around to Harley sitting alone on the deck. He got up to go be with him. Kitty rose and followed Scott, who paused before he opened the door.

"How is he?" Scott asked softly.

"I don't know. Jett and Harley were like two parts of a whole. It was as if they were connected—like twins." Kitty's voice quivered as she wiped her tears.

"And you?" Scott gently touched her shoulder.

"Jett was my fix-it man when it came to problems with Harley, and now he's gone forever. My friend ..." Kitty gulped to contain a sob as she gazed out at Harley. "But Harley—I'm so worried about him. Jett affirmed all that was good in Harley, and Harley did the same for Jett. Harley loved him dearly. Jett was part of his soul. Now he's gone, and my husband is alone."

Scott understood. He went out into the cold to talk with Harley. It was quiet on the large deck with its view of the hilly landscape, thick with trees. The icy wind was blowing bitter cold, but grief had taken away all feeling for Harley.

"May I join you?"

Scott drew a chair up close and sat. Harley began talking as he looked at the lawn as if he expected Jett to appear at any moment.

"Just Saturday afternoon we played football over there for hours." Harley pointed and then held up a grass-covered sweater. "I found this on the dryer. He was wearing it. I can't imagine never hearing Jett's voice or seeing his face again."

Scott patted Harley's arm. "I understand. I can't replace him, but I'm here for you."

"Thanks, you do understand, don't you?" Harley replied. "Did they tell you that they identified Jett's body at the crash site? We got the call just a couple of hours ago."

"No." The horrible nightmare was confirmed.

Then Scott remembered how Jett got him to talk after Alex's death. He looked at Harley and said, "Tell me about Jett—your memories."

"I owe my life to Jett." Harley turned to Scott. "I've never told anyone this, but I planned to kill myself when I got back to prison. The full scope of my years of sin finally hit me. You've heard the big items, but there were hundreds of little ones, such as telling the girls I'd be there for a dance recital but not showing up or calling until several days later.

"Legally I had numerous felonies against me over the years, and one more would have sent me to a maximum facility. I figured suicide would set the ones I loved free from the shame I had brought them. I even had a backup plan.

"On the way back to the prison Jett told me how much my dad believed in me. His words were like a fire to my soul, because I had abused my dad's trust. On top of that I couldn't bear the thought of being locked up for the next three years. Six weeks had already seemed like an eternity. As I walked over to Jett for a final good-bye . . ." Harley looked over at Scott, and his sigh was full of pain before beginning again.

"Jett could give me a quick hug on the field when I ran a touchdown, but never for any real reason because he felt showing that sort of affection wasn't manly. But that day, he stepped out of his comfort zone and hugged me like Daddy did when he wanted to give me courage—an intimate, soulful hug. I decided if God could change Jett, then maybe he could give me the strength to truly transform my life."

"You're telling me that from the risk Jett took with his manliness that you were willing to trust God?"

"Exactly. Jett never did anything without thinking how it would look to others, but that day he only worried about me being able to hang on. Jett restored my hope, and it's because of that I'm alive today."

ে৵ ে৵ ে৵

Standing at the graveside, Scott thought about what Harley had said and the people who had risked everything for him. The decision he needed to make was becoming clearer.

Too quickly the service was over. Clark closed his Bible. The men from Mississippi quietly sang "Take My Hand, Precious Lord" as Clark spoke with each member of the Taylor family. An exhausted Donna kissed her husband's coffin and walked toward the car that would take her back home. As she passed Scott she took his hand.

"Could you come by the house tonight around eight? I've got something for you." With that she was gone from the cemetery.

ে৵ ে৵ ে৵

Samuel rode with Scott to Donna's house. Neither of them had much experience driving on snow, especially on the winding back roads. Donna answered the door dressed in blue jeans and Jett's red plaid flannel shirt. Looking very thin and pale, she hugged both men as they stomped snow off their shoes. Music was playing in the background.

"Thanks for coming. Samuel, my father is in the kitchen. I'm taking Scott to the study."

Donna motioned to Scott. They walked down the hallway to a large room with relics of football days past. He sat down in a crimson leather chair next to a lamp, the only light in the room. Donna sat on the footstool and held out an envelope.

"As you know, Jett's briefcase was found intact. When I opened it, I found some letters, one of which was to you. If it's okay, I'd like to talk with you before you open it."

"Go ahead." Scott held the letter like it was a fragile egg.

"Jett told me you were uncertain about what direction you should follow in your life."

"I'm very angry with God about Jett's death," Scott said.

"I don't know why Jett had to die when things had just turned around for him spiritually. Our marriage was improving and he was becoming a good father to our son. However, God knew that plane was going to crash. He could have intervened, because this old briefcase certainly made it through. God chose to allow Jett to die.

"While in the last five months Jett's life came together spiritually, ironically he went to Pittsburgh because of those changes. If he hadn't confessed to Alex, he'd have become unbearably rigid like his father. Life isn't predictable, Scott. When you and Jett had lunch, you had no idea in three days he'd die. Putting off a decision about what you're going to do with your life is actually making a decision. Please, go ahead and read the letter."

Tears brimmed in Scott's eyes as he read:

My dear friend,

Please do not take this note as my attempt to make a decision for you; however, let me encourage you to reach with both hands for what is eternal. We discussed many 'what-ifs,' but the rewards of this Earth do not compare to what God has for each of us when we cross the finish line.

We're here to carry you through the uncertain times when the journey becomes too hard. I pray for you daily and want you to know that you'll always have support when you need it. You are a

*most special friend and I desire to see you fulfill all God has called
you to be.*

>*My love and support,*
>*Jett*

"It's like he knew he was going to die," Scott said.

"Maybe he did."

He looked at Donna and thought about her words before speaking.

"I need to make a phone call, and then I'd like to see my father."

Ten minutes later Samuel entered the room and sat where Donna had
been earlier. Scott handed him the note, and after Samuel read it, he asked,
"What can I do?"

"I've just made a call authorizing the sale of my business. Once I get the
details squared away, I'd like to go back to Austin with you—not just for a
holiday visit, but for an extended time. Could you come back to Atlanta with
me, and then we'll go home together?"

Samuel didn't have to think before he nodded.

35

CHRISTIAN WOMEN'S CLUB MEETING
JUNE 1, 2007

"THAT WAS THE BEGINNING. The events I've told you about here tonight had an impact on each of our lives beyond our imaginations. I challenge each one of you to see people through God's heart—a heart of grace." Annie stopped and smiled at her audience. "I thank you for your time. I will now address any questions."

Several hands went up, and Annie pointed. "Yes, the lady in pink on the third row."

"How did your family suffer once life got back to normal?"

"It took an extremely long time for us to recover. Nursing an AIDS patient is emotionally and physically exhausting. It's not only a catastrophic illness but a disease with an enormous stigma. We all suffered because of it. I went from senior honors English teacher to teaching the ninth grade. The decision came from the board of education, and their reasons were logical, but realistically it was an unjustified demotion. Many of the people who pushed for my job change were longtime friends of the family. In all honesty, it was difficult to forgive and let go. Eventually that happened for me.

"Forgiveness was even harder for the boys. Ben was shunned by his baseball team, and he was understandably upset. Thankfully, Ben's college team had excellent coaches, and now he's quite successful as a professional baseball player. The guys who sent Brian the package continued to torment him for several years when he would be home during holidays. He really never looked back even though it was difficult to endure such things. That summer of 1994 inspired his life's work—caring for AIDS orphans in Africa.

"The Linder family paid their respects after Scott left, but they believed we were wrong in bringing him into our home. It's been thirteen years, and we haven't done much more than speak cordially since Alex's death—it was their choice to distance themselves from us. Next question, please. Yes, the gentleman in the last row." Annie sipped water.

"Did Scott ever marry? What happened when he went to Austin?"

"Over the last decade Scott has made some critical decisions about his life choices." Annie stopped, looked at Wayne for a minute, and fished for words. "It's much too long to tell tonight, but I thank you for your question."

Annie smiled as she asked for one last question.

For the last hour Wayne had watched the man in the back of the large banquet hall. Even though the lights in the room were dim, Wayne could tell he had been wiping tears from his cheeks as Annie spoke. No one around him paid any attention. It was the first time Scott had heard Annie speak.

Wayne's thoughts shifted back to Annie as she was finishing.

"In closing I'd like to quote Mother Teresa: *Loneliness and the feeling of being unwanted is the most terrible poverty*. Ladies and gentlemen, we've got a mission field with our family, friends, and in our communities. We are God's hands to give someone food and drink, to be a friend to strangers, and to visit the sick. As we do that we open the door for them to know he cares. People—gay, straight, sick, or well—need to know that Jesus loves them. Thank you so much for inviting me."